Aayat Athar finds herself in an alternate dimension. She is saved by cousins Feedaa and Sae Sae, who inform her that she has landed in Faejenda, a city occupied by Djinns. They offer to help her find a way back. Sae Sae's father was a researcher who has crossed the interregnum—the pathway joining the dimensions—and is now stranded in the human world. By helping Aayat, Sae Sae wants to reunite with his father.

A few Djinns in Faejenda, looking to open a permanent portal to the human world, are declared unruly by the government, and live in a community outside the gates of the city.

Feedaa's mother, Errumm, is the district head, and along with her team, she is planning an attack on the Djinns who love humans side. She is aided by Tenzen, a recently transferred, and his secret partner.

Aayat, Sae Sae, and Feedaa begin exploring the disappearances of others to understand the ways the crossover works. Meanwhile, Sae Sae secretly meets the human lovers, who ask him to bring them the details of the siege planned by Errumm and her team in return for the information about the interregnum.

Beyond the Interregnum
Copyright © 2023 Nazia Kamali
ISBN: 978-1-4874-3868-5
Cover art by Martine Jardin

Published by eXtasy Books Inc

Look for us online at:
www.eXtasybooks.com

Beyond The Interregnum
The Other World 1

By

Nazia Kamali

CHAPTER ONE

Aayat looked at the ceiling with half-sleepy eyes, wondering if the day had dawned. Sucking in a sharp breath, she traced the bed to find her mobile phone to check the time. She was not ready to wake up yet. The fabric felt peculiar as she swept her fingers over it. Her skin sent an alien sensation to her brain. She had never touched something like that before.

Aayat snatched her hand away in horror.

It banged against the frame of the bed.

She bolted upright. *My bed doesn't have a frame.* The sudden rush of blood to her head made her dizzy. Sleep vanished from her charcoal black eyes in an instant. She blinked them repeatedly to adjust to the prevailing semi-darkness and peered around.

She was in a wide cavity-like room with no windows. Countless devices sat around her. Some of them beeped and blinked, their monitors displaying indecipherable content. The absence of proper light made it look like she was in an ill-maintained hospital, but it didn't smell like one—no pungent smell of chorine or bleach or blood. In fact, the room seemed neutral in that respect, no smell at all. Aayat focused her concentration on listening to the noises in her vicinity, but other than the beeping, there were none—no distant chatter, no click-clack of shoes, no sound of any movement whatsoever.

The air around her felt strange—sterile—as if she had been suspended in a vacuum.

Goosebumps stood out from her skin as panic rose in her throat. *Where exactly am I?*

Shaking the fear that had engulfed her being, calming her fiercely thumping heart, Aayat gathered her wits. She had to get out of there. With trembling legs, she got up from the bed and leaped towards the entrance, but weak as she was, she stumbled and fell on the floor. Somewhere an alarm blared loudly, and someone ran in.

Strong hands picked her up and placed her on the bed again. "Don't try to move," a robotic voice said, booming across the room.

Aayat raised her head. A tall girlish-looking creature with a slightly crooked nose and long cylindrical limbs smiled back at her. "Hello, I am Feedaa."

It has a name?

"Are you all right? You look like you have seen a ghost. The concern underlying the creature's robotic voice confused Aayat further.

She kept silent, looking at the creature with narrowed eyes.

"Say something." The creature prodded her and said, "Can you speak? I hope you speak."

"What are you?" Aayat moved towards the edge of the bed.

"Who, the correct word is who." The creature corrected Aayat in the manner of a grammar teacher teaching her pupil different parts of speech.

"Huh?" Aayat looked at it, bewildered. Her breath became shallower. She swallowed with great difficulty, the dryness in her throat becoming imminent.

"You should ask *who you are* and not *what* . . . And I already told you I am Feedaa." The creature placed its hands on its hips and tilted its head.

"Not your name, I am asking what are you—robot? Humanoid? Or a new invention by some crazy scientist?" Aayat eyed the bizarre creature with suspicion. It was tall—about six feet, with turquoise-coloured eyes, full lips, skin that resembled that of humans, and no hair on its head. It smiled at her with what looked like genuine affection.

"What's a humanoid?" the creature came closer and asked.

"Where am I?" Aayat inched further away, maintaining a distance of few feet between them.

"In my cousin's lab."

"Why?"

"Because we brought you here," the robotic creature replied, shrugging its broad shoulders.

"How can you have a cousin?" Aayat squinted her eyes.

"Why can't I?" Its words sounded more like banter than a response to someone's question.

The urge to hit that strange thing swelled in Aayat's mind. "I need to leave," she said, placing her feet on the floor in urgency.

"No, no, no, you can't." The creature placed its hands on Aayat's shoulders, applying great pressure to keep her seated.

"Why?" Aayat widened her eyes, crushed under its weight. Was she being held hostage? This could not be. She was no one important—just a regular scholar who had shifted to Dehradun a few weeks back. She hadn't completed any worthwhile research yet, nor was her mentor working on a secret project that she knew of. She was no rich man's daughter, either.

Absentmindedly, Aayat lifted her hand to scratch her head, but the creature shouted, "Don't. The detectors attached to your scalp will fall off. As it is, we had a lot of trouble attaching them because of the outgrowth."

"Why would you do that? Why? And what, what are you trying to achieve?" Aayat ran her long fingers through her hair frantically, trying to dislodge the detectors. They could not experiment on her without her consent. She was not a lab rat.

"Hold, hold. What are you trying to do? You cannot do

that." The creature grabbed her hands in one swift motion and tugged them away.

Aayat struggled to reclaim her hands—she twisted and twirled with all her might, but she was no match to the creature's strength. The dimly lit room turned darker before her eyes. Her brain stopped responding for a few seconds, directing all its effort to prevent her system from collapsing.

Gradually the creature loosened its grip and brought a chair near Aayat's bed.

"Breathe… Breathe . . . Why are you so scared? I am not going to harm you," it said, trying to soothe her.

What's happening? Where am I? Why am I here? Who are you? What do you want? Aayat's mind swirled with questions.

An annoyed expression passed the creature's eyes. "I am Feedaa. This is my cousin's lab. He and I were hiking in the woods when we saw you lying unconscious near the stream. We tried waking you up, but you wouldn't budge. There was no identification card on you, so we were left with no other choice but to bring you here. Leaving you to become animal fodder didn't feel kind."

"Where is here? I mean, which place?"

"Faejenda, you are in Faejenda."

"This isn't Dehradun? Did the stream carry me somewhere far away?" Alarmed, Aayat stiffened in her place. The vein near her temple pulsed vigorously. "I should get back, I need to get back. Can you please help me get back?" she pleaded in a soft voice.

"Where do you live?"

"National Centre for Research in Artificial Intelligence campus."

"National Centre for Research in Artificial Intelligence?" Feedaa repeated the words and narrowed its eyes. It then blinked repeatedly as if trying to remember something.

"You can, right? You can help me get there. Just call them and ask if any Aayat Athar works there. They will tell you all about me. Please, just help me out."

"Why don't you rest a bit first? As soon as you can walk, we will take you there," Feedaa replied and stood.

As the creature neared the entrance of the cavity, Aayat called from behind, "Why didn't you take me to a hospital? You could have left me there. The authorities could have easily traced my address. Why bring me here?"

"Rest up. We will talk more when you feel better." Feedaa walked out of the room, leaving Aayat to ponder over her words.

The place turned colder, as if the temperature had dropped by several degrees right after Feedaa left.

Aayat sat on the bed motionless, bracing herself tight, racking her brain, trying to recall the events of the day. One minute she was walking by the stream, the next, she was lying in this alien place. She tried hard to remember what happened in between, but nothing came to her mind.

Her body felt tired, dragged downwards by the weight of overthinking. She lay back on the pillow and drifted off to a dreamless sleep.

CHAPTER TWO

When Aayat came to her senses again, the lights had turned dimmer. It was still cold and quiet, but her skin seemed to have adjusted to the ambient temperature. She looked around to see if the creature had returned. Instead, she found a plate full of fruits on the side table. Despite all her reservation about the place, her stomach growled loudly at their sight, and she began gorging on them.

"Woke up already?" Feedaa had waltzed into the room without notice. Her outfit had changed. She looked like something of a cross between a rock star and a farm girl.

Aayat was suddenly ashamed of the way she was devouring the fruits. A little while ago, she'd questioned everything she was told, and now she was eating the fruits most probably brought by Feedaa.

Feedaa laughed at Aayat's blood flushed face.

How could a robot laugh like that?

"How are you feeling now?" it enquired.

"Better, thanks," Aayat replied, trying to hide a half-eaten apple between her fingers and palm.

"Excellent," Feedaa said, clapping its hands and resting its hips on the corner of the table at Aayat's bedside.

"What happened to sending me back?" Aayat sat upright on the bed and looked at Feedaa with eyes like that of a little lost puppy.

"Well . . . umm . . ."

"What?" Aayat raised her eyebrows and craned her neck in Feedaa's direction. All her doubts returned.

"We are looking into it." Feedaa looked sideways, concentrating on the indecipherable content the machines were displaying.

"What's there to look into? I work at a public institution. It's not like I'm asking you to send me off to a distant cave. Just call me a cab and I can take it to the institute. You don't have to pay or anything. And as for the treatment bills, send them to me and I will wire the money online. Now please let me go." Aayat got up to leave, but Feedaa stopped her again, and just like last time, she was no match to Feedaa.

Contrary to Aayat's expectations, Feedaa's touch was warm and soft. Although it gripped her hands tight, the touch wasn't cold or harsh. Aayat eyed Feedaa with contempt as the creature seated her again on the bed.

"Your name is Aayat, right?"

"Yes."

"Aayat, please let me run a few diagnostic tests. Once I am sure that you are fit and fine, I will let you know what's happening."

"What tests? You already have these small paper-like things attached to my scalp, your machines are beeping, taking note of my every breath. What more do you want to test?" Aayat withdrew from Feedaa. Her jaws tightened as she tried to huddle herself in a ball.

"I just need to draw some blood from your arm to check your kidney function and blood count. Once that's done, we can have a long chat." Feedaa coaxed Aayat to calm her down.

"I don't want a long chat, nor do I want you to draw any blood. I will not allow this. This is an invasion of my privacy, and I can file a criminal charge in case you do that forcefully." Aayat felt nauseated. She would have run outside by now had Feedaa not blocked her way.

"Listen Aayat, we need to talk, and I can only do so after my work is done." Feedaa spoke firmly.

"And what exactly is your work?" Aayat raised her eyebrows.

"To make sure that you are back to normal again." The creature had already collected the required instruments while holding Aayat with one hand.

"Is that supposed to be a joke? Because I don't find it funny at all. Why would you worry about my health? What is it to you whether I live or die? I don't know you, you don't know me. Let's cut this nonsense out and go our own ways." Aayat raised her voice and wriggled under Feedaa's grip, which had tightened in the meanwhile.

"I am not the enemy here." Feedaa's whispered entreaty, her mouth quite close to Aayat's ears, shocked her.

"Then who is?"

"Everyone else."

This remark silenced Aayat. Something lurched inside her stomach as she turned limp for a moment.

Feedaa loosened the grip.

"I know it is very difficult for you to trust me. I wouldn't trust myself either in similar situation, but at least give me the benefit of the doubt." Feedaa's robotic voice had a soothing undertone.

"First remove all the detectors, shut down the machines and the cameras and then I might be willing to listen to what you have to say." Aayat reclaimed her nerves and pointed to the electrodes attached to her scalp.

"Fine, I will remove everything except the bug in your ear." Feedaa slid off the table, walked to the nearest machine, and turned it off.

"I have a bug in my ear?" Aayat jumped off the bed.

"Yes, and it needs to stay put or you won't understand what I am saying."

Aayat looked at the robot with a mixed expression of disgust and bewilderment.

"We speak different languages, and this bug helps with the translation, so that you and I don't have any problem while conversing with each other. I am also wearing one." Feedaa pulled out a minute, wireless device, the size of a small pebble, from their right ear, showed it to Aayat, and put it back in place.

"How did you get it out?" Aayat slapped her ears with her palm, trying to dislodge whatever Feedaa lodged in her ears. She shook her head vehemently, but to no avail. She then looked at Feedaa, who giggled and winked.

Aayat exhaled sharply and sank lower at her spot. A certain numbness overtook her body. She looked at Feedaa, but she was unable to see anything beyond a robotic creature creeping closer.

What had she gotten herself into?

Feedaa placed a hand on Aayat's shoulder and said, "Don't look like that. I am not going to harm you or anything." It then came around and sat on the bed. Softening the voice, it continued, "Keep calm, relax, I am, I mean we are, well, this place… Just know that I am not going to harm you. I promise. Believe me."

Aayat's head was still bowed. She put her hands in her lap and scratched the cuticles of her fingers as Feedaa kept speaking. "Just listen to me with an open mind. You told me you are a scientist, so I believe you have a broad understanding of the world and its dimensions."

She raised her head to look at Feedaa. "What do you mean by that?"

"When you slipped into that stream, you were somehow carried away from your world and landed into ours. This is an alternate world where humans *do not* exist."

Blood drained of Aayat's face as Feedaa kept speaking.

"This is planet Earth, but the dimension you are in at the moment is the one inhabited by other beings. I am sure you must have read about us like we have read about humans." The room spun before Aayat's eyes. She held the side of the bed to prevent herself from falling backwards. Goosebumps jumped all over her hands as the air enveloping her turned colder.

Then, as if to give Aayat some time to absorb the information, Feedaa got up, walked up to the entrance, looked outwards for a while, and returned. "I know it is difficult to understand, but it *is* the truth. And for now, I will leave you with this. We will talk further once you wrap your head around all this." With this Feedaa got up to leave but Aayat stopped her.

"Do you really want me to believe all this?"

Feedaa passed her a black, smooth-edged rectangular remote, the size of a wristwatch dial. "Raise the screens on the walls when you are ready and look outside. I am sure it is markedly different from the views you are used to seeing. I know, I really do, that it's almost insane to think that you have suddenly landed in a different place, but the sooner you accept this, the easier it will be for you."

Right before leaving the room, Feedaa turned and said, "And by the way, I am a *she*. A female."

Aayat looked at her and then at the remote. She was new to Dehradun. There were hardly any landmarks that she remembered. She had no idea what to expect when looking outside the window. Nevertheless, she pointed the remote towards the opposite wall, but there was no button. Confused, she touched the surface of the remote, hoping that the touch screen would be activated. Again, nothing happened. The shining upper surface glowed upon her touch, but the light died soon. Aayat slapped it like she did to her television remote, and again the surface glowed with the same intensity; however, nothing else happened. She flipped the remote and slapped the opposite side. It didn't even glow.

Frustrated, she threw the remote on the bed and got up.

She needed to do something—move, work, occupy her hands—anything to keep her from going crazy.

Feedaa's assertion about not being human buzzed in her head.

That's impossible. Someone must be feeding that robot meaningless chatter.

She automatically put her hands to her ears. This time she could pull the plugs out, so she removed them and threw them on the floor. The absence of a pair of slippers was painfully evident as she used her bare feet to somehow smash the plug into pieces. She then inspected the room. The bed frame seemed like it was made of wrought iron or a similar metal. A table stood nearby, also made of wrought iron, minus a chair. She had no watch to know what time it was, and she barely remembered the day of the week. It was probably . . . Thursday.

The devices kept in the room were unlike the ones she had seen in her lab. They were smaller in size, seemed lighter, and their exterior was made of an unknown shiny material, which, contrary to her expectations, felt warm to her hands. The walls of the room were warm to touch, too. None of the devices was wired. Small blinking lights on their sides told the observer if they were working or not.

These devices might be fitted with a camera.

Aayat was suddenly very aware of her every move. Slowly she crept back into the bed, scared to even twitch the wrong way.

They must be watching me.

A few minutes later, the wall in front of her began to change colour. Fluorescent light flooded the room, as the wall glowed like the screen of her laptop when switched on.

Aayat tried to leap into a flight, but her body wouldn't obey. Fear had swallowed her. Her eyes and jaws twitched and the pulse of the vein near her temple quickened, but she stayed rooted on her spot.

A hologram-like, three-dimensional image of Feedaa materialised before her eyes into the empty space between the bed and the wall. It smiled and said something. This time the voice wasn't robotic but feminine. However, the language was gibberish. Aayat couldn't make a word out of it. The hologram laughed and moved its hands, pointing in different directions, but everything sounded alien to Aayat's untrained ears.

After a while, the hologram stopped speaking. It just stared at her in continuation. When Aayat did not respond for some time, it pointed towards her ears.

Is it asking about the ear plug?

A few moments later, the hologram vanished, and the wall returned to its usual colour—a dull shade of hay.

Feedaa didn't know I crushed the earplug. She wouldn't have spoken so much otherwise.

A smile spread across Aayat's face. Her heart danced jubilantly. It was her chance to flee.

She dashed towards the entrance like a fawn saving itself from deadly predators and crashed into the opening. The rectangular space in the wall through which she had seen Feedaa enter was not an open door. It was hard—solid. Crashing against it hurt every joint of her body. She stayed on the floor for quite some time after the fall. A flood of pain shot through her body.

Slouching on the spot where she had fallen, she held her breath for people to rush in and scold her or tie her or scare her in any way to make her obey, but no one came.

Aayat began crying. She wailed, but no one listened to that, either. Her stomach felt leaden as she thought of the trap she had fallen into—strange land, strange language, weird people, and no knowledge of how to get back. Gulping in the cold air, she tried to calm herself down, but nothing worked. She hobbled back to the bed and kept leaking tears until she was exhausted.

No one knew her in Dehradun. She usually called her parents once in a week. She had no friends either, so how would anyone know she had gone missing? Will they even look for her? By the time the news of her disappearance had reached her parents, it would be too late.

The more she thought, the more frightened she became. Her body trembled like a dried leaf and her heart throbbed in her throat. She jabbed her forehead with her fingers, forcing herself to think of a way out of the situation, but nothing worked.

Exhausted from the feeling of not belonging, she huddled her frame into a dark corner of the room and kept sitting there for a long time. There was a knock on the transparent entrance that she couldn't cross but Aayat never bothered to see who it was.

A gibberish noise coming from close by disturbed her self-isolation. When she raised her head, Feedaa was towering over her sulking form, speaking in an unknown language. Her right hand was extended towards Aayat, and the left was flying in the air making undecipherable gestures.

Not knowing what else to do, Aayat took the hand and got up. Feedaa led her towards a wooden chair, probably taken from another room, and produced another ear pod from her pocket. Though a little sceptical, Aayat took it and placed in her ear.

"That's right. You need this to understand what I am saying. And what havoc did you create here? Sae Sae came and knocked at the door for so long. When you didn't respond, he checked the footage and called me. I came rushing as fast as I could. What happened?" Feedaa said so many things in a single breath. "What happened, Aayat, tell me."

"Didn't whosoever it was who came knocking at that strange door see in the camera what happened?" Aayat snapped.

Feedaa laughed out loud and kept laughing for a long time, shaking her head in continuation.

"Oh my god. Whosoever it was who came in knocking. Sae Sae is going to fume at the nickname. You are so funny Aayat. I like you already."

Aayat frowned at the strange creature standing in front of her. How could she laugh in such an annoying fashion?

Oddly, something at the back of Aayat's head nudged her to trust Feedaa. She had suffered no harm in the many hours she had spent at the place, nor had she been hurt while unconscious. Although she was tired and her body felt sore in places, it was because of the fall and not their doing. Feedaa had removed the electrodes as she asked, and whoever knocked earlier had the decency of not entering the room without her permission.

Aayat decided to go with her instinct. She had to go home, and for that, she needed information. She needed to know everything about where she was, who the owners of the lab and Feedaa were, and what they wanted.

Mellowing her expressions, Aayat spoke in a mild tone, "Feedaa, I don't understand anything. Nothing makes any sense to me. Can you please help me?"

"Of course I can, but as I said earlier, you need to keep an open mind and trust that whatever I tell you is true."

Aayat nodded in response. But as soon as Feedaa opened her mouth again, the wall changed colour and another hologram materialised in front of them.

"Feedaa, hide that human now. Ray is here and I don't want her to see the human. Hide her *now*."

Without any warning, Feedaa took Aayat's hand and rushed her towards a corner of the room. She then lifted her right hand and mumbled some instructions. A hollow cuboid made of thin, slippery sheets descended from the roof and covered them on all sides.

"Just keep quiet for a few minutes please," Feedaa whispered.

CHAPTER THREE

Feedaa held Aayat's hands as they stood motionless, enveloped in the dark, cold, hollow cuboid. She thought about what Feedaa had told her. They were not in Dehradun, but some place she hadn't even heard of.

Faejenda . . .

Faejenda . . .

Faejenda . . .

The name churned in Aayat's mind until she heard a knock.

"Come out. Ray is gone."

Feedaa whispered something into the chip fitted to her wrist, and the cuboid unsheathed them into the open space of the room.

Once her eyes adjusted to the sudden burst of light, Aayat noticed the creature standing in front of her. His features resembled Feedaa's—crooked nose and no hair on the head—but with ocean blue eyes and a face that oozed smug confidence as opposed to Feedaa's friendly appearance.

Feedaa introduced the creature standing in front of them. "Aayat, this is Sae Sae, my cousin, the owner of this lab and a grade one lunatic."

Sae Sae bowed a little.

Aayat tipped her head in return.

"He is the best person to direct all your questions to," Feedaa said, looking at the other creature, then at Aayat. "His dad spent his life researching the existence of humans, so he has a better idea of how to start and what to tell." Rubbing its eyes, Feedaa continued, "Sae Sae, she wants to know more about…you know…us, here, everything, and honestly, I don't even know what to tell her or where to begin."

Researching the existence of humans, what does that even mean? Aayat narrowed her eyes as she looked at the other creature but remained silent.

"Fine." Sae Sae turned and led them from the room they stood in to the inner sanctum, separated by a thin, slate-coloured, floor-to-roof, soundproof sheet made of a seemingly fibre like material. Aayat raised her hand to touch it but then decided against it and scuttled behind Sae Sae.

The study was stacked with huge piles of papers and files. Several crumpled papers and broken chips were strewn all over. In the middle of the room was a round table surrounded by several chairs of different shapes and sizes. Leaving them at the table, Sae Sae went towards the cupboard in the right corner of the room and returned with three small transparent bottles with magenta coloured liquid filled up to their neck.

Aayat looked from Sae Sae to the bottles to Feedaa and then looked at Sae Sae again. Did they expect her to take the bottle and drink? How could she be sure that it wasn't anything harmful? However, Feedaa snatched one of the bottles from Sae Sae's hands and gulped the contents in one go.

These creatures eat and drink like humans?

"Go on. I am still alive, aren't I?" Feedaa nudged her, placing the empty bottle back on the table.

Aayat touched the bottle, then pulled her hands away. Sae Sae smirked and leaned backwards on his chair, but Feedaa unscrewed one of the bottles and placed it in her hands firmly.

The cool liquid tasted sweet with a minty aftertaste. Her body relaxed and her mind felt freer. It didn't swirl with questions and doubts anymore.

Sae Sae pushed the other bottle towards her, but Aayat shook her head.

He then cleared his throat, "How much did Feedaa tell

you?"

"A little." Aayat spoke timidly. "Ummm…I am in Fae-jenda, a city in the alternate world, occupied by what we call non-humans." She looked at them and pursed her lips.

"Correct," Sea Sae said and nodded. "Do you believe it?"

"No, but I have no other option."

"Do you trust us?" he asked.

"No, but—"

"You don't have any other option." Feedaa spoke this time.

"Yes." Aayat placed her hands on her lap and stared at them.

"Then you need to make up your mind. Either you trust us, or you don't." Sae Sae's tone was devoid of any common courtesy. "You have been here for almost three days now, we haven't hurt you, and we do not intend to." He wasn't as welcoming as Feedaa. His square shoulders were tense and rigid. His eyes seemed cold, and the air between him and Aayat felt dry. Listening to him speak sent fearful sparks down Aayat's spine.

"Hmm," Aayat responded, getting weary of the introductory session. She wanted to fast-forward the conversation to the point where she was told the information about leaving this place and returning to her world.

"What do you gather by non-humans?" Sae Sae traced the lid of the unopened bottle with his index finger.

"Umm… I don't know, I thought you were robots but… Feedaa just drank that whatever it was so…" Aayat shrugged her shoulders.

"Robots?" Sae Sae looked at her quizzically.

"Well, machines with artificial intelligence that help us perform daily chores with ease."

Sae Sae scoffed and looked at Feedaa and then back at her, "Djinn. We are Djinns and not some machine, and this dimension is called…"

Aayat shrieked, "Djinns… really. Djinn… I mean … I thought… really? Like the one Aladdin found in his lamp?"

Feedaa, who had been silently listening to the conversation for quite some time, asked, "Who is Aladdin?"

"So you have heard about us?" Sae Sae raised his head, his piercing gaze landed on Aayat's face.

"Some people believe in your existence, or so I have heard."

"Then let's not waste any more time on this and get to the point. This is my father's lab. His work revolved around documenting the human ways of life in your dimension. He is the reason we have these ear pods."

Aayat opened her eyes wide. "Documenting human ways—wait! So you people believe in our existence? You weren't sceptical about our presence?"

"We already had proofs, and my uncle went to your dimension twice. Our whole world believes that humans exist," Feedaa replied.

"So I am a lab rat?"

"A lab what now?" Feedaa blinked her eyes.

"You brought me here for further research." Aayat's nose flared and her blood seemed to rush through her body at twice its usual speed.

Sae Sae closed his eyes and shook his head. "Insolent creature. We put our neck on the line to save you, and this is what we get in return. Accusation. We brought you here because no one comes here. I use this place for my personal experiments, and, except Feedaa and Ray, no one ever sets foot inside the threshold of this lab. And you accuse us of trying to experiment on you? You must live in a very untrustful world, or probably you are an untrustworthy creature. People seem to think of others what they themselves are."

Clearly alarmed at Sae Sae's irate behaviour, Feedaa jumped in quickly and said, "We had to hide you because our people don't like outsiders. There was no other choice."

"*Don't like* is a polite expression for what we feel," Sae Sae glowered. "Most Djinns accept that there are other beings on the planet but want to have nothing to do with those beings. As it is, I don't see a point in saving you, either. How easy was it for you to blame us?"

Aayat dabbed her forehead with one of the crumpled papers lying on the table. It felt rough against her skin, but she had no choice. She couldn't wipe her face with the sleeves of a borrowed dress. She then cleared her throat before speaking. "You don't like humans, you don't want to know them, your people are going to torture me to death if they find about me, you two saved me, and I am grateful for all of it. Now tell me, how do I go back?" Sae Sae was telling her everything except what she wanted to hear.

Both cousins looked at each other, their faces changing expressions every second.

Sae Sae licked his lips. "That I don't know."

"You were acting like such a know it all and you don't know this? And after being so clueless, you expect me not to be suspicious?" Aayat slammed her palm on the table. Her head began spinning as if she was on a high-speed Merry-go-round.

Sae Sae roared, "Listen, you ungrateful human, this is my place, and I am granting you protection because Feedaa wanted to. If it were up to me, I would have left you to become animal fodder. It would have been good riddance."

"Is this the way you usually talk to everyone?" Aayat retorted.

"Yes, you know why? Because I—"

"Let's take a break." Feedaa dragged Sae Sae out of the study.

All the fear that had left her because of Feedaa's polite behaviour came rushing back in. Aayat's teeth chattered and her limbs trembled. Once again, she was covered in goosebumps, and the hair on the nape of her neck stood firm. She placed the soles of her feet on the edge of the chair and, burying her head between her knees, hugged herself tightly. The empty room echoed Sae Sae's words about not knowing how to send her back.

Someone put a blanket on her from behind.

"Don't mind him. He is a nut case." Feedaa's voice reached Aayat. "We will find a way out. I am sure. And he wouldn't have left you there, even if I wasn't by his side." Some of the warmth from Feedaa's hands and words flowed into Aayat's body. "He is just angry because he fought with Ray, his fiancé. That's all."

Aayat raised her head. "You really don't know how to send me back?"

Feedaa's turquoise eyes avoided Aayat's. "No."

Aayat exhaled sharply and buried her head between her knees again. Feedaa placed a hand over her shoulder and patted.

Moments later Sae Sae returned. "I am going to look for ways to make you leave. We don't want you here anymore than you do."

Feedaa scolded her cousin. "Why do you have to be this rude? Can't you see she is scared?"

"Shut up, Feedaa. I am in no mood for a lecture."

Feedaa ignored his words and continued, "Ray stomping out of here was your fault, not Aayat's. Stop treating her this way."

Sae Sae came closer. Aayat could sense heat radiating from his angry body. "You will stay in this lab, and you will stay low. You will not do anything. Don't touch anything, don't move anything. The only thing you are allowed to do is breathe. If you follow that, there will be no problems. In the meanwhile, I need to run some errands. And Feedaa, you better go home, your mother thinks I am a bad influence," he ordered.

"That you are," Feedaa said, grinning.

For the first time, Aayat saw Sae Sae's lips curve upwards in a smile.

Once he was gone, Feedaa brought out a small black flat-surfaced device, not larger than a one-centimetre cube, from one of the drawers of the table, and handed it to Aayat.

"What's this?" Aayat rubbed her thumb over the device. It was smaller than the remote Feedaa had given her earlier.

"Communication Device."

"This small? How do I use this?" Aayat asked, turning the device every way around.

"I have fed our identities in this, mine and Sae Sae's. You can communicate with us by asking the device to connect you."

"How?"

"Bring it closer to your mouth and speak my name and it will initiate the connection. When I receive and accept the offer of communication, my hologram will materialize in front of you, and we can talk. There are hosts of other functions in this device, and I trust you to find all of them by the time we meet again." Feedaa smiled and got up. "I don't know what you like to eat or what food you have in your world, so for now, I have brought some fruits. I saw the pictures in my uncle's journal. I will bring something better from our kitchen tomorrow. And rest well. I know it is a lot to process, but the sooner you accept the reality, the better it will be. And don't be scared, I am just a call away."

Feedaa was smarter than Aayat had originally thought. "How old are you?" she asked.

"Seventeen sun cycles."

"Seventeen years old," Aayat repeated.

Feedaa nodded. "Yes, I think that is the correct

translation."

"What do you do?"

"I am studying to be a—what do you call it in your world? I don't know… ummm… I would be saving the planet from dying if I succeed." She clumsily patted herself on the back.

"Environmentalist." Aayat smiled.

"Okay. Now I need to hurry, mum will be home any minute. And don't worry, tough guy is not going to hurt you. He just pretends to be harsh. Sleep tight. *Hofta.*"

Feedaa walked out of the room, leaving Aayat to ponder the information.

Chapter Four

Sae Sae slithered through the narrow, pothole-filled, serpentine streets of the dangerous area at the opposite end of the city. The dilapidated walls on either side were painted red, with slogans defying the government, blaming them for targeting those who thought differently. The security cameras were smashed, and most streetlights were unlit. The criss-crossed power lines hung loosely, almost touching his head.

A small tunnel separated the zone from the main township. The area that opened on the other side was occupied by human supporters, those who championed free intermingling with the human world. From about a century earlier, they had been working towards the goal of opening a direct portal into the alternate dimension, and to the alarm of their government, the supporters were increasing in number. Since the government had stopped developing the area in order to curb the advances, most of the buildings in the area had crumbled. Plaster had fallen off the walls, revealing old bricks. Boundaries were half-broken and wild bushes had sprouted everywhere they could take root. The stars twinkled brightly above, making the absence of streetlights less noticeable.

At a sharp bend across the intersection, a steep wooden staircase ascended to the upper floor. Sae Sae took the steps to reach a poorly lit room with a black termite eaten wooden door hanging by the hinges. Above it hung a homemade sign—*Human haters and government lovers not allowed.*

He touched the door, which creaked open. The room was occupied by four beings. Three of them sat around a rectangular wooden table, playing cards, while the fourth occupant sat on a chair near the window on the left wall of the room, looking outside. The sole bulb in the room, hanging by a frayed cord a few feet above the table, flickered noisily. Two moths buzzed around it.

One of the Djinns, with two half-broken front teeth, called out as the other two joined him, laughing, "Look who we have here. The mad voice artist."

"I am here to discuss business," Sae Sae snapped.

"You are always here to discuss business but never get anything done," the Djinn with broken teeth replied, kicking out a chair for him to take a seat.

Sae Sae glared at him, stepped inside the room, and sat on the other chair at a distance from them. "I need a way to go to the human world." He looked at the Djinn by the window through the corner of his eyes. It was his first time seeing him. He scrutinized the new addition with curiosity.

The plump Djinn, with deep seated eyes and wearing a dark blue t-shirt over black pants, remarked instead of the first one, "We have known that for quite some time now."

Sae Sae pursed his lips to stop himself from replying. The plump Djinn's outfit appalled him enough to make him want to vomit.

"There is a price to everything. You know that, right?" The first one cocked his head.

"What do you want this time?"

"Your aunt is preparing to make this city free of our group. Get us the plan." The third Djinn sitting immediately across from Sae Sae tapped his fingers on the table.

Sae Sae's senses revolted at the sight of his dirty fingernails. "I haven't seen her in ages."

"Her daughter comes to your lab every day." The first one came extremely close to Sae Sae's face and grinned, baring his ugly yellow teeth and bad breath.

"Deal with me." Sae Sae banged his palms on the table.

The fat one replied calmly, "We are dealing with you. Give us what we are looking for, and receive the map to the human world. It's a pretty simple exchange."

Sae Sae got up so fast his chair fell backwards with a loud thud. His nose flared and he stomped out of the place without saying anything. His blood felt as if it boiled in his veins as he walked all the way towards the lab.

When his father had disappeared seven years ago, Sae Sae believed he was stuck in the human world. Abee had been to the human world twice and had returned each time, unscathed. Sae Sae had thought he would come home this time, too, but when three months passed, he became worried and tried every method he knew to open the portal to the alternate world, but to no avail. After failing for the umpteenth time, around two years ago he turned to human lovers. They passed on the information in instalments. They told him about the interregnum, the pathway that connected the two dimensions and how people got lost in it all the time. However, they hadn't yet told him how to open the portal or cross the interregnum safely. They tested him several times before providing each bit of information and kept doing so each time he returned.

Sae Sae hadn't told anyone about his interaction with the human lovers, not even Feedaa. She was twelve years his junior and yet somehow had become his closest friend over the past few years. He knew that she would never accept his contact with these people. Naughty as she might be, there was a line she wouldn't cross.

But he needed to find a way to make Aayat go back where she came from. Her presence was getting on his nerves. She reminded him of his father, who might be in a similar situation somewhere—trapped, scared, and unable to do anything, at the mercy of strangers. Who knew what kind of people he had met there?

Errumm shot an angry look at her as Feedaa entered the house. "Where are you busy these days, Feedaa?" She stood right at the entrance, dressed immaculately in a crisp white shirt, navy blue slacks and a matching coat, checking the time.

"Sae Sae's lab," Feedaa replied meekly.

Errumm and Feedaa looked similar except for the age wrinkles that lined Errumm's temples and the corners of her mouth and eyes. There were a few brown age spots on her neck and the back of her hands, matching the colour of her eyes. She was as tall and had the same broad shoulders and hips.

"Why? What illegal experiment are you two conducting now?" Errumm asked, glaring, still blocking Feedaa's way with her towering frame.

"None. We are just hanging out together, thinking about what I should do for my finals, you know." Feedaa tried weaselling her way past her mother, who finally stepped aside.

"Study. Why don't you try studying for a change? I think that would work perfectly well in the finals." Errumm placed her hands on her hips. The frown on her face accentuated the lines on her forehead.

Feedaa changed the subject, "What's for dinner?"

"Why don't you set up a kitchen in that god-forsaken lab?" Errumm spoke through her teeth.

"Why do you hate that lab so much?" Feedaa slumped on the sofa, placed a cushion on her lap, and squeezed it tight.

"As if you don't know that. It is anti-government to look into ways to contact humans. Also, I am worried about Sae Sae. That boy is obsessed with his father's research. He left such a lucrative career and took to hiding in that lab. I am tired and worried, and now even you are giving me headaches." Errumm placed her hand on her forehead and sat beside her daughter. Her shoulders drooped as she exhaled audibly.

Sae Sae was her brother's son. Feedaa knew she loved him like her own. However, he never listened to what she said. After his father's disappearance, he'd left his studies midway and retreated into a shell. Errumm tried hard to force him out, but nothing worked.

"Sorry, Mum. I didn't mean to do that, but you know how lonely Sae Sae is. With uncle and aunt both gone, he is all alone. We are his only family, so I go to keep a check on him every now and then. And I think he doesn't get along with Ray these days, either. There is constant bickering and fights. He doesn't love her." Feedaa placed her head on her mother's shoulder and her hand over the other one.

Errumm's features brightened a little under her daughter's comforting touch as she said, her sarcastic side returning, "Sage Feedaa, will you please concentrate on your own life?"

"Sage Feedaa . . . You are so funny, Mum." Feedaa doubled up with laughter. "How come people don't see this side of you?" She ringed her arms around her mother's neck.

Errumm smiled, her anger mellowed by Feedaa's laughter.

"Come, let's have dinner." She got up, smoothed her pants and walked toward the kitchen.

"Mum, can I please pack a few things for Sae Sae? He hasn't had a good meal in ages. All he survives on is the food that he makes, and you know how that tastes." Feedaa ran after her mother, flapping her arms like an overgrown chicken.

"Sure. Now please eat and go back to your studies. And no parties until the finals. How come you don't get tired of those flashy get-togethers?" Errumm placed two platters laden with vegetables blanched in sea salt, pepper, and oil with a few slices of flat spinach bread on the platform and gestured

Feedaa to drag two chairs that lined the windowsill.

"You have become old, Mum. *Tch-tch* what a pity," Feedaa chimed in, and received a smack on the head in return.

Feedaa's world revolved around two people, Errumm and Sae Sae. She knew nothing about her father except that she got her turquoise eyes from him. She often pestered Sae Sae to tell her more, but his lips remained sealed. Instead, Sae Sae took a place in her life which seemed like a cross between a father and a brother. They leaned on each other in times of need and tortured one another on happy days.

After helping Mum with the post-dinner chores, Feedaa went to her room.

Littered with new, used, unused, and worn-out things, it looked like a museum. There was hardly room for anyone to set foot on the floor without toppling down or ramming into the antiques.

A round black wrought-iron bed sat in the middle. Golden flower and bell motifs were built into its head rest. The spring-coiled branches from the edge of the head rest on each side interlaced together at the centre. Flowers with large petals and broad leaves protruded from the branches and decorated the head rest. The bed had been built by her grandfather and had originally belonged to Errumm. When Feedaa saw it for the first time, she shrieked with joy and asked her mother repeatedly to let her have it.

The right corner of the room had a wooden three-tiered rack stuffed with tattered, yellow-paged books. Though all material was available in digital form, Errumm often suggested Feedaa read hard copies—*you connect with books and content better when you hold the thing in your hands and leaf through each page.*

Feedaa's virtual calendar occupied the wall opposite the one with the wooden rack. It displayed the schedule for her classes, sports activities, community service, and parties that she was invited to. An alarm buzzed before each event. The same wall served as her screen for displaying texts and assignments. The space between the wall and her bed was left empty to allow the characters from real-time videos to materialise and play. The other two walls were plain white.

Kicking the ball that had rolled out from nowhere, Feedaa walked up to the centre of the room and jumped on her bed. She then removed her contact lenses and set them aside. Although they served as her communication device, information surfer, and played videos, music, and lectures, she hated wearing them. The lenses had a detector embedded in the software. Errumm could check her whereabouts whenever she wanted to by using a passcode that she refused to share with her daughter.

Staring at the ceiling, Feedaa thought about Aayat's situation. It was bad. They had no idea how and when the portal between the two worlds opened, what triggered the transfer, or how they could send Aayat to her world. It might be several solar cycles before she could go back.

When Sae Sae's dad disappeared, he'd searched for him like a maniac for almost two years before coming back to his routine life. And even then, he kept working on the notes his father had left so that he could find a way to the alternate dimension. In those seven years, he lost his mother, his life, and his laughter.

Feedaa hated to think that someone on the other side of the portal could have also been waiting for Aayat the same way, not knowing what to do, what to expect, or when and how to move on. She hated to see Aayat trapped in a place where she knew no one. And the worst part of it all was that their world was anti-human. Most Djinns hated intermingling with the humans and would never leave Aayat alone if they got a sniff of her presence.

It was frightening.

Feedaa shut her eyes tight. She'd had a busy day and

wanted to get some rest, but the scary thoughts about Aayat and her future wouldn't stop churning in her mind. Giving up on sleep, she sat up straight with her back resting on the head rest.

She had access to the security footage of Sae Sae's lab, so she instructed the chip she usually wore on her wrist to play it in two dimensions on the wall of her room. Frame by frame, she began analysing every corner to make sure Aayat was safe. For the first time in her life, she realised how fearsome it was to not know exactly what was going on.

Sae Sae retraced his steps back towards the lab and went straight to his father's study. He then displayed some notes on the table and begun reviewing. They included a detailed map of the jungle. After discovering Aayat, Sae Sae believed that the stream flowing in the midst of the jungle was one of the links, and to his relief, he saw that it fell under the jurisdiction of the administration.

He spread out the map and studied it closely, trying to recall the exact location where they'd found Aayat. He wished they could have taken her to the stream, but that was not possible in broad daylight.

Seven spots on the map were circled in red with *probable zone* written on them. Sae Sae murmured a command into the chip on his wrist, and a virtual, rotating nine-dimensional version of the map materialised before his eyes. He sliced the model according to the seven probable zones his father had marked, enlarged the one with the stream, and began navigating through that part of the jungle virtually.

The study in his bunker was approximately six hundred square feet in area, too small for even the small subsection with just one zone to spread evenly, but it was the only safe space he had.

Sae Sae passed every tree, gazed through each stone, and looked around each bend with utmost care. Scanning through the winding dirt roads, he tried to understand the characteristics of the area. There had to be a reason why his father had marked and labelled them.

It was a daunting task, walking through the nine-dimensional holographic model repeatedly, looking through the same trees and bushes. His eyelids drooped and his back and shoulder blades ached. The day had already been taxing. He felt as if his neck would snap in two at any moment.

He took one last look at the video feed from the room Aayat was in to check if everything was all right and, seeing she was okay, went to sleep.

Looking for a way to the human world was a marathon, he told himself. No one could do it in a single day.

CHAPTER FIVE

For a moment, Sae Sae's steps froze at the sight of Ayaat in his father's study. Her eyes were narrowed, her lips were shut tight, and the long, dark brown strands of her hair were spilled all over her shoulders. She scratched her forehead and bent closer over the old paper map Sae Sae had dug from some old, tattered book the previous night.

"What are you doing here?" he roared.

"Looking for something to do. I can't just sit here and wait," Aayat replied without looking at him, moving her index finger through the map as if trying to trace a path.

"Where do you think this is? And how did you enter this room?" Sae Sae snatched the map from her hand, almost crumpling it to pieces in the process. It was his sanctum, the only place where he felt his father's presence. No one dared enter the room without his permission, not even Feedaa.

"Well, you brought us here last—"

"Get out." He pointed at the door.

Aayat sat there, staring back at him, her oval, charcoal black eyes opened wide.

"Didn't you hear me? Get out. *Now.*"

Aayat's face and ears burned red, and her nose flared. She bit her lower lip, got up, turned on her heels and stomped out of the study. Her ponytail lashed behind her.

Aayat slammed her fist on the side table before sitting on the chair in her room. The remote Feedaa had given her fell on the floor due to the commotion, and the screen of the opposite glass wall slid open. Bright golden sunlight streamed in, blinding Aayat. She raised her hand to her eye level and peered through the shade. For the first time in four days, she saw daylight.

Maybe it was the psychological effect of knowing that she was in an alternate universe, but the light blue sky and sunlight felt unfamiliar. It was beautiful yet alien. The skyline seemed tilted, and the sun seemed to be of a different shade of yellow—brighter and more piercing than she was used to seeing. The buildings rising to towering heights surrounded by well-chiselled trees looked like strangers one met on public transport—similar yet unknown.

Entranced by this suddenness of her encounter with the outside world of this alternate universe, Aayat forgot to take note of Feedaa's entry.

"What are you looking at?" Feedaa placed her hand noiselessly on Aayat's shoulder. Aayat jumped and looked sideways, making Feedaa erupt in laughter.

"You scared me."

"Mission accomplished, then." Feedaa elbowed Aayat to make room for her and sat on the table. "I love to do that," she said with a wink. "Wow, you looked like you saw a ghost."

"Of course I saw a ghost, that mad cousin of yours—"

"Yeah, he is quite close to being one intimidating devil." Feedaa looked around. "By the way, where is that devil?"

"When did you come here?" Aayat asked, smoothing down her ponytail, bringing it over her left shoulder.

"A few *twinks* earlier."

"I am so glad you did. It's so scary here, being all alone. I don't know how I will survive this place. And when you aren't around, it becomes even scarier. I feel so lonely." She had now wrapped a few strands of hair on her index finger and was twirling it.

"But Sae Sae has been here all the while. He hasn't gone home in four days, lest you should run into some danger," Feedaa replied innocently.

Feedaa's words amazed Aayat. He didn't look the caring kind. With those fiery eyes and the scalding words that came out of his mouth as soon as he opened it, he was more of a haughty animal in her eyes than a humble Djinn.

"Well, he is kind of scary to talk to. He is angry all the time. Every second of the day. All he does is glare at me as if I would evaporate from the heat of the spark of his angry eyes."

"That he does," Feedaa agreed, nodding as she placed two bags on the bed in front of Aayat.

"What's this?"

"One has food, and the other has some clothes for you. It's been four days. You need to change. Sae Sae doesn't like sharing clothes, so you can't continue to wear his." Feedaa tugged at the beige jacket Aayat wore over black pants.

"Can I eat first? It's weird. I don't do anything at all, and yet I feel tired and hungry. My stomach keeps growling, it's embarrassing." Aayat placed her palm on her stomach.

"That's probably your body responding to the travel through the interregnum. I remember reading in uncle's notes that it tires one out." Feedaa shrugged.

"Interregnum?" Aayat sat beside Feedaa.

"Oh, the path that links the two worlds."

"And by uncle, you mean Sae Sae's father?"

"Yes, he was my mother's brother—is, he *is* my mother's brother," Feedaa replied, averting her gaze. "Let me call Sae Sae, he must not have eaten either." She got up and left.

Aayat sighed and rested her chin in her palm. There was so much she didn't know. Everything happened within the blink of an eye. She hadn't even realised she was drifting away from one dimension to the other. *How is it even possible to drift across the path? How come I don't remember any of it?*

Feedaa returned with Sae Sae and opened the packets of food. They arranged themselves on the bed around the food.

"This is *eostro,* chickpea cooked with wild goose. I don't know if you eat such things, but this was all I could manage. And Sae Sae, Mum was asking if you still have a job, or have you decided to become a total *keefe*?"

"*Keefe*?" Aayat raised her eyebrows.

"Waste of a person," Feedaa replied, laughing.

Sae Sae fumed at her.

"Eat, eat, and tell me if you like it." Feedaa slid the food towards Aayat, who devoured the food, putting it in her mouth so fast that she almost choked. The food was delicious, and it seemed like she was having a proper meal after an eternity. From the corner of her eyes, she saw both Feedaa and Sae Sae smirking, but couldn't care less.

Feedaa passed a cup of water towards her. "Here, drink some water. Don't choke yourself to death with food. It isn't a glorious sight."

Aayat snatched the cup and guzzled the liquid in one go. It tasted different.

"This is *water*?" Aayat placed the cup on the side table.

"What else would it be?" Feedaa waved the bottle at her.

"It tastes different." Aayat licked the corner of her lips.

"How different?"

"Well, umm, it's sweeter. Doesn't water taste bland? You know, sort of no specific taste, but this is quite tasteful, I must say—"

"We have work to do. Finish up fast."

"Why are you such a buzz kill, Sae Sae?" Feedaa crinkled her nose.

"Why are you so relaxed when we have to take care of this alien species?" Sae Sae snapped.

"That's just disrespectful. You can't talk about someone like this. Have you never learned manners?" Aayat spoke before Feedaa.

"Are you not, then?" Sae Sae shot angry looks at her.

"I am, but you don't have to make it sound like an abomination." Aayat wiped her mouth with one of the crumpled food wrappers. Feedaa had forgotten to pack tissue papers or anything similar.

"Abomination." Sae Sae's lips curled upwards as got up from the bed. He walked towards the glass wall and peered outside before speaking again. "No, I don't think you are an abomination, but you are not one of us, either. And your presence is endangering us. The longer you stay, the worse it will become. So all I want is for you to return to your world so we can put this incident behind us and move forward with our lives."

Aayat looked at him and nodded. For the first time in the four days that she had known Sae Sae, his words made sense.

"What do you propose we do, then?" Feedaa asked.

"You, my cousin, need to go back to the academy to prepare for the finals, and we adults will handle the matter on our own. As it is, your mother thinks I am a bad influence. If you fail your exams, her words will prove right, and that is not something I want."

"But I want to be here. I am also a part of this. And I am not a baby, I will soon be an adult." Feedaa stomped her feet.

"We can and we will. He is right. You need to go back to your studies," Aayat replied instead of Sae Sae.

"You can't possibly side with him. You said he was annoying. And he says you are a waste of his time," Feedaa protested.

"I appreciate your concern Feedaa, but we will handle ourselves." Aayat gave her a polite smile.

"Now get going." Sae Sae lifted Feedaa by her arms and dragged her towards the transparent door.

"Where do we start?" Aayat asked, once he returned after

showing Feedaa out.

"Come to my father's study after you change." Sae Sae left the room, taking the trash and leftover food with him.

Aayat rummaged through the bundle of clothes Feedaa had brought. None of them was like what she was used to wearing, but having no other option, she chose a crème coloured full-sleeved sweater and a navy blue skirt. There was no comb. She smoothened her hair with her hands and tied it neatly in a bun before going to the study.

When Aayat entered the study, Sae Sae was hunched over the table at the centre. A small portion of the virtual map of the jungle rotated in front of him. It looked as if part of the jungle was floating mid-air, hovering a few inches above the rectangular table. Each tree, each rock and pebble was visible. The stream that flowed in the middle of the jungle, gurgled through the map. Around it were the eucalyptus trees, minus the sweet syrupy smell.

She stood at the opposite end of the rotating map. Sae Sae grunted in response and handed her the crumpled paper map he had snatched from her hand that morning. "This is the map of the jungle where we found you."

Then pointing towards a red-coloured cross marked near the stream, he told her that they found her somewhere around there. Seven small circles were marked in black. Aayat studied the marks and placed her fingertip on one of the black marks, "What are these?"

"I don't know. Abee marked them."

"Abee?"

"My father. He was working on finding a way to open the portal to your world when he disappeared. He must have found something interesting at those places or maybe they are the places he tried and failed. I don't know. Everything is a guess, now that he is . . . not here." Sae Sae's sentence made Aayat uncomfortable. She looked at the map for a while, scratched her brows, and then cleared her throat before speaking. "This rotating map is a part of the jungle? It doesn't look complete. Is it the only part with the stream? You have sliced the map in parts?"

"Yes. Why?"

"What are you trying to find?"

"Way to send you back," Sae Sae replied without looking up.

Aayat chuckled. "Is that the only thing you think about?"

"You have left me with no other choice." He looked at her and smiled. The frown on his face was smoothed by the effect of the curve on his lips.

"Any leads yet?" she asked, lighting up in response.

"Let's walk through the stream." He dragged the table towards one corner of the room, motioning Aayat to do the same with the chairs to clear space for a portion of the map to materialise. He then rotated the map using his hands so that the stream flowed diagonally and murmured some instructions.

The surrounding trees with a hint of mountains visible at a distance took shape around the stream. Wind blew through the virtual map, swaying the leaves of the trees and affecting the direction of the waves rising in the stream. The temperature of the room increased as a fake sun shone overhead.

"This is the closest we can get to it. Now let's walk. Do you remember the path you took the day of the incident?" Sae Sae looked at Aayat, who shook her head and took a few steps to come and stand beside him.

"Does this stream look familiar to you?"

Aayat kept silent.

"Let me add a few more attributes. You might remember something then."

He projected the trees, bushes, and rocks on the walls, giving the map the characteristics of the surrounding forest. A few virtual birds flapped and chirped overhead. Small insects whirred and buzzed around them, creepers crawled over the trees and covered the floor along with the dried leaves and broken twigs. It looked like an exact replica of the forest once Sae Sae was done, but to Aayat's dismay, she still could not remember anything.

To avoid disappointing him, she enquired about the place they'd found her and suggested retracing their steps from there.

He looked at the paper map and marked the virtual map by placing a cross near a giant tree with hanging roots. "Here," he said.

Aayat walked towards the point and then marched from there towards the end of the stream and back, then towards the other end of the stream. Sae Sae made her walk until she lost count how many times they traced the bank of that virtual stream. She was covered in sweat, strands of her hair stuck on her face. Her feet ached with so much walking and she panted, trying to keep up with Sae Sae's pace. Her palms felt sticky; she wiped them continuously on Errumm's skirt that she was wearing. Few sweat droplets trickled over hey eyelids and onto the lashes before she cleaned them with the back of her palm. Her entire being felt smudged. Still she kept dragging herself.

"You still don't remember anything, do you?" Sae Sae asked, coming to a halt at the edge of a virtual rock.

"No."

"You are one dumb scientist." He flicked his hand and the map disappeared. He then brought two chairs and two bottles of water from the corner of the room. Offering Aayat one of the bottles, he took a seat opposite her. Aayat waited for his forehead to develop deep frowns, but it didn't. He rolled the sleeves of his shirt and placed his hands on his knees, looking sideways.

The walk they'd taken in that room had somehow loosened him up.

"You aren't disappointed or angry?" she asked in a quiet voice.

"I am. I definitely am," he said, turning to face her. "But there is no point saying the same thing over and over again. It won't make you remember anything."

"I'm really sorry for putting you and Feedaa in this position, but I really don't remember anything. I wish I could, God knows I do." Aayat placed the bottle on the floor and wiped the corner of her moth with her thumb.

Sae Sae waved his left hand and said, "I don't think people remember how they cross the interregnum. Abee thought so, too. He was—he is a smart man. He would have found a way back to me if he remembered the path. He had gone to your world twice and returned, however, he never remembered how he came back. Someone must have helped him." His face turned small, the light in his eyes almost disappeared and his aura darkened in an instant. "Where is that someone now?"

"I am sure he is still out there, trying his best."

"I hope so, too."

Aayat leaned forward and squeezed his arm.

Chapter Six

Sitting on one of the chairs in the study, untangling the locks in her hair, Aayat saw Sae Sae enter. She quickly pushed a lock behind her ear and straightened.

Sae Sae sat on the chair at the farthest end of the table and picked one of the research papers from the pile.

Aayat broke the silence. "I am Doctor Aayat Athar. I work at the Artificial Intelligence Centre where my mentor and I are working on a robot that can make the lives of people suffering from Parkinson disease easier."

"What?"

"Well, I thought we should introduce ourselves formally," Aayat replied, extending her right hand.

"Oh. Yeah." Sae Sae shook her hand lightly. "I am Sae Sae, as you already know. These days I lend my voice to smart machines to earn a living."

"But that's not who you actually are?" Aayat looked at him sheepishly.

Feedaa's absence had somehow made the two lower their defences. With no one to mediate, they were forced to talk to one another without animosity.

He nodded.

"Then, who are you? What do you do? I mean Sae Sae the person, not Sae Sae the part-time voice artist." Aayat played with a lock of her hair, winding it on her index finger.

"What is it to you?"

"I need to know who I am entrusting my life to. Don't I?"

"What if I don't turn out to be trustworthy?" Sae Sae

reclined on the chair, his arms crossed over his chest.

"I see, you don't trust people. You keep responding to my questions with questions as if to avoid divulging information. Why is it so? Why don't you trust people? Did something happen?"

"Do you?"

"Do I what?" Aayat arched her eyebrows.

"Do you trust people easily?" Sae Sae's lips curved a little as he ended the question.

Aayat laughed at his words and moved her head towards the right. "See, this is what I'm talking about. You answer questions with questions. Anyways, is this all your father's?" She pointed at a box placed on the table.

"Do you know what's inside?"

"Things that look like microchips. I know I shouldn't have, but I peeked. I was curious to know why you wouldn't allow anyone in the study." Aayat bit her lower lip. "Are you angry?"

"Will my anger stop you from doing anything like that in future?" Sae Sae cocked his head.

"Your father must be one hell of a man...Djinn... um...no... AaDjinn. And I mean that in a good way." Aayat raised her hands up, palms upfront in a defensive manner.

"He sure was." Sae Sae smiled. "By the way, what disease are you working on?"

"Parkinson's."

"Parkinson's?"

"It is a degenerative disorder, where people lose control of their motor abilities. The Central Nervous System is affected, and muscles become rigid, making it hard for people to do chores that involve physical articles."

"Got it." Sae Sae lightly drummed his fingers on the table.

"Don't tell me you have already cured it. I see your machines are quite sophisticated." Aayat looked around the room.

Sae Sae filled her in, still talking as if he were in a dreamy haze. "Not cured, but we do have early detection to reduce the effects as much as possible. Also it's called *Eorough* disorder here."

"What are you thinking?"

"Nothing."

"You get that lost in thinking nothing?" Aayat stretched on her chair.

"I'm thinking of the similarities in our worlds."

"No, you weren't." Aayat shook her head.

"How can you be so sure about what *I* was thinking?" Sae Sae almost poked a hole in his chest with his index finger.

"You were thinking about something difficult and emotionally complex. Your face almost contorted and you weren't making eye contact like you usually do. Your eyes weren't focused, and—"

"Don't you get tired of overthinking?" Sae Sae threw a paper map at her. "Study and process if you have such a burning desire for analysis."

Aayat caught the paper and asked, "What do we do next?"

"Take you out of here. You must be feeling stuffed." Feedaa chimed from the entrance. She half walked and half skipped to reach them. Her eyes shone with mischief.

She came and sat on a chair beside Aayat.

"It's high time, Sae Sae. Let's introduce her to our world. Who knows, we might never meet again. Why not make the most of it?" Feedaa's hands as usual were flying mid-air, supplementing her excitement for the cause.

Sae Sae jumped from his chair in chagrin as he said, "You want to take her out for a ride?"

"Why not?" Feedaa spread her hands sideways, palm upright.

"For starters because everyone will know we have a

human with us, and you know what will happen after that." His blue eyes showed a tinge of red at the corners.

"Then we will make sure no one knows she is a human. Just look at her, she seems fine dressed in Mum's clothes. She can move perfectly well, she is well mannered, seems well-bred. What more do you want?" Feedaa then turned towards Aayat, "I am sure this non-emotional being hasn't told you yet, but you look gorgeous."

"Feedaa, you are out of your depth. You don't know what you are talking about." Sae Sae's tone was hard crusted.

"You are the one who doesn't know how to have fun. Aayat, don't you want to get out of this place? I know you do. Don't be scared of this moron. I am here to protect you from him. If left to him he—"

"Why are you talking so much, Feedaa? The human will get tired of you pretty soon."

"Aayat. My name is Aayat, not *the human*." Aayat opened her eyes wide.

"I like you, Aayat, I really really do. Someone needs to scold Sae Sae exactly the way you do." Feedaa clapped her hands, looking like an overgrown child in her tall frame. Her eyes had a sparkle that made Aayat want to trust her without a peep.

Sae Sae dragged his cousin out of Aayat's earshot and whispered, "Why are you making things even more difficult? Don't give that human any wrong ideas. We cannot take her out of here. You know the drill, we need identification cards wherever we go. Besides, she looks different. Why do you always look for ways to cause a ruckus?" His lips quivered with anger.

"Because she needs to go to the jungle to recall exactly what happened. Maybe, maybe she could remember something and lead us towards the portal. We need to give her that chance, Sae Sae. She must want to go home." Feedaa's tone softened him a bit.

"It will need a lot of preparation. She needs to blend with us. We can't risk her standing out," he warned.

They went back to the study, where Aayat was busy examining the map included in one of Abee's research papers. Sae Sae could see it explained how the natural features of the two worlds were alike, but the boundaries of districts and towns were marked differently. It also consisted of a topographical map marking the similarities in features. He wondered if she even understood their language. "Why do you keep rummaging through my things?" Sae Sae bellowed.

"Because I need a way out," Aayat shot back.

"Now, now, let's not start the quid pro quo again, please," Feedaa said, sliding an arm across Aayat's shoulders.

"Before we take you out, we need to give you a few details about the world you are in."

Aayat nodded and crossed her legs, keeping her hands on her right knee, one above the other.

Feedaa began filling her in. "This is the town Faejenda, as you already know. I think we have almost the same anatomical and physiological structures as humans,"

"We don't have that stupid outgrowth on our head here," Sae Sae intervened. He was now sitting on the floor in a dark corner of the room beside the book rack, from where he carefully studied Aayat as he tried to figure out what was hidden underneath. He always had a hard time trusting people. When he'd introduced Ray to Feedaa and Errumm, both couldn't believe that he had finally found someone he wished to spend his life with.

"Yes, we need to do something about that. But other than that, we look alike. As I already said, physiological features are the same, and I don't think anyone is interested in knowing people on an anatomical level in first meeting, so that won't be a problem. So the females are called AuDjinn and the males AaDjinn. What else? Yes, a body of administrators runs the town, and every person has an identity pass issued by the admin office. Our language is—"

Sae Sae spoke from the dark corner of the study, cutting her off. "*If*, if we go out with you and anyone asks, you are unable to speak. We will tell them that ever since she heard some shocking news, she has stopped speaking. This will end all the issues with language."

"I thought you were not interested in taking her out."

"Will you listen if I say so?" Sae Sae snorted and looked at Aayat, who was chewing her lips ferociously.

"My mother hates when someone does that." Feedaa looked in the direction of Sae Sae's gaze and spoke. "Your lips are going to bleed badly at that rate."

"Sorry, I was just listening." Aayat placed her hands on her lips and stiffened. "What if someone asks who I am?"

Sae Sae rubbed his face with his hands and closed his eyes. He then stood up and paced the room, his hands held together at the back. "My mother had a friend who died in a fire accident. We will say you are her daughter."

"Which friend? Why have I never heard of someone like that?" Feedaa raised her face, chin protruding outwards as she questioned her cousin.

"Because I am telling it to you now. Stop annoying me, Feedaa."

"You have any more details? I need to know who I am impersonating." Aayat squinted.

"She lived down south. Her house caught fire three years ago. She and her husband passed away in that fire. They had a daughter Zenzee, who died when she was nineteen, but her parents never registered her death." Sae Sae's voice wavered. Tears stung his eyes. He had known Zenzee since they were kids.

"That's sad, but would work perfectly to our advantage," Feedaa said quietly.

"Fine then, let's do it." Aayat got up and smoothed the dark-brown pencil skirt she was wearing with an off-white blouse. "What do we need to do to make me more like an AuDjinn? However, I am telling you, I will not shave my hair. Never."

Sae Sae mouthed the words *your problem* and rummaged through his stuff, watching them through the corner of his eyes.

Feedaa asked Aayat to stand and then circled around her, looking at her from her head to toe. She then brought the bag of clothes and emptied it on the table before them. When nothing came to her mind, she scratched the back of her hairless head and drummed her fingers on her lips.

Aayat sorted through the package Feedaa had brought the previous day and brought out a length of fabric.

"Why did I bring that?" Feedaa examined the piece.

"It's good that you did. I can use it as a scarf, see." She wrapped it around her head, covering all her hair.

"You look stupid." Feedaa blinked.

"We can say I burnt the side of my face and some parts of my head in the fire. It looks ugly, and hence the scarf."

"People undergo surgeries here—they don't become a candy with a wrapper around them." Feedaa crinkled her nose.

Aayat arched her eyebrows high and asked, "You have a better idea?"

Feedaa scratched the tip of her nose and shook her head.

Aayat stepped under the sun after what felt like an eternity. Her skin lapped up the warmth readily, and it spread throughout her body. The pores of her skin opened to absorb the feeling. She rubbed her palms on her arms and inhaled with all her might. Her lungs felt overjoyed. She repeatedly took deep breaths as if to fill in all the fresh air she could. Finally—something familiar.

A long metallic road lay flat in front of her. To its other side were gigantic trees full of yellow flowers in full bloom. Behind them were more trees. As far as Aayat could see, it was all green—no people, no buildings, no vehicles, just trees. A light breeze blew across her face. It smelled like lilac. The sky above was spread wide, its blue soft on her eyes. A few stray mackerel clouds floated in between the crowns of the higher trees.

Her communion with nature was broken by Sae Sae's noiseless arrival in a deep blue car that hovered about a foot above the ground. He lowered it to let them in.

"Come on, let's go," Feedaa said, leading her towards the car, and opening the door of the back seat.

The inside was furnished like a lounge, with leather-covered seats and enough legroom to spread one's feet wide. It was cold and smelled like citrus punch. *Definitely Feedaa's choice.*

"What are you looking at?" Feedaa turned backwards and asked.

"What does this car run on?"

"The concept of magnetism. If you know what it means," Sae Sae said in a mocking fashion, then continued as if proving Aayat's inability to understand the concept, "You know the process where the semiconductors are charged at room temperature. It decreases the frictional loss and increases efficiency and output."

Aayat looked at the back of his hairless head from her seat, wanting to spit out the rest of the process to show she understood it, but she kept quiet.

The car sped into a frictionless, bump-free ride at one hundred and fifty kilometres per hour, until a uniformed man with a protruding belly and dull yellow eyes stopped them. His wrinkled face looked tired, and he walked with heavy steps.

"Is that you. Sae Sae?" he asked.

"Yeah, going hiking," Sae Sae said, clearing his throat.

"Towards your grandmother's trail?"

"Yes."

"How many times a week are you going hiking these days? Is everything all right?" the man asked with a fake concern, his voice discerning.

"Just a little bored," Feedaa replied instead of her cousin.

"Who is the other AuDjinn?"

"Old friend from down south." Sae Sae's annoyance was clearly noticeable in his voice.

Chapter Seven

In a dimly lit, dingy room at the corner of street number 12.1, three aadjinns sat around a circular table. One of its legs was broken, and bricks were stacked in its place to provide support. Amoeba-shaped patches covered the surface of all four walls of the mould-infested room.

"What happened to the Aadjinn who came for information about the interregnum?" the Djinn with a slash on his right cheek asked, speaking in a husky voice.

"Nothing," the one with a red bandana on his forehead replied.

"Why did you let him leave that day? What if he brings people from district administration over?" the one with the slash snarled.

"He won't."

"How are you so sure?" the Djinn with a slash rubbed his right eye with the back of his palm.

"His father has crossed the interregnum. He is desperate to bring him back."

The third one, who hadn't spoken anything until then, sat up straight, the chair creaking under his weight as he shifted. The other two turned towards him, but when he kept drumming his fingers on the table, they went back to their discussion.

The silent one's communication device buzzed, and he went to the window to check the message.

Smiling, he came back to the table and said, "We will have the plan in our hands by the next full moon."

"How?" the aadjinn with bandana asked.

"I know someone in the administrator's team."

"And he is going to just hand over the plan to you?" Slash-faced cocked his head.

"You are not the only ones who wish to freely intermingle with my world." He grinned and scratched his shaven head.

The one with the bandana asked, "Then why did you ask that voice artist to bring you the plan?"

"To cross-check. This is not the first time I am going up against the authorities. It is what made me cross the interregnum in the first place." He grinned.

"You must have been a dangerous man in your world, Jackal." Slash-faced laughed and thumped Jackal on his back.

A series of trees rushed past Aayat as the car self-drove into the jungle. She looked at the green blur with awe. It reminded her of a family trip to Andaman and Nicobar islands. Her father had made up for not being there for her fourteenth birthday by taking her to the islands for a week. Aayat had been overjoyed—the evergreen trees with broad leaves covered ninety percent of the land, making it almost look like a green tent in places. They'd gone underwater diving and on a jungle safari, smelled the overcrowded vegetation that filled her lungs with joy, and eaten local sea food—cuttlefish, red snipper cooked with coconut—to her heart's content.

The car halted noiselessly in front of a clearing and lowered. Its doors opened and the occupants stepped out. The bright golden sun beamed overhead. Aayat placed her hand over her eyes to protect them from the glaring sun, feeling the lack of sunglasses. A dirt trail with well-marked fencing on both sides led toward the trees in front of them.

Feedaa pointed towards a sign posted on the left side at some distance. "Welcome to the trail of Kausar."

"What?" Aayat looked in the direction Feedaa pointed.

"This is one of the most popular hiking trails around the region. It seems deserted because it's the peak of summer and the middle of a working day. You must see it on holidays or during a better season. It's literally crawling with Djinns," Feedaa explained.

The cool fresh air with its leafy smell and the clear sky above made Aayat feel welcomed. Aayat wanted to remove her scarf and let her hair loose, allowing the breeze to run through it, but fearful of Sae Sae's reaction, she kept it covered as it was.

This might not be such a bad experience after all.

"Walk and talk," Sae Sae instructed, peering around to make sure no one was following them. He wore a white cotton t-shirt with black pants and a cap, and had a brown leather bag strapped to his back. He was alert, continuously looking towards the right and the left to avoid any mishap.

Feedaa broke a branch from one of the trees, removed its leaves, and gave it to Aayat to use as hiking stick. "This trail is named after our grandmother. She was a, what did you call it? Enviromental . . ."

"Environmentalist."

"Yes, that. Amji loved nature. Every morning she would come to the jungle to make sure it was doing all right. I saw very little of her, but I am telling you Aayat, she was one hell of an AuDjinn. Smart, courageous, fierce. No one stood a chance in front of her." Feedaa plucked a leaf from one of the bushes and gave it to Aayat. "Smell this. Isn't it amazing? When Amji was young, very few of these trees remained, so she started a crusade to save them. At first there was very little support, because people just didn't listen to her, but slowly everyone came to their senses. Now they grow around the jungle in abundance."

"What about your grandfather?"

"Amja? Oh, he was a cool aadjinn, he owned a metal craft

workshop. What beautiful designs he created. None of us got that artistic ability." Feedaa giggled and continued, "I will show you his workshop someday when mum is not home. It's still there in the basement."

"So your Amja worked from home while your grandmother crusaded?"

"Yeah. Why?"

"Nothing, it's just—" Aayat bit her lips and fell silent. Her parents had shared a very different relationship. Her father's work had always dominated their lives, leading to exhausting fights between her parents, which made her distrustful of partners.

A few strands of hair threatened to come out of her scarf. Sae Sae narrowed his eyes as she tightened the cloth.

"Stop. We are not going this way," he said, coming to a sudden halt, blocking Feedaa's path, extending his arms.

"Why?" Feedaa almost fell due to inertia of her movement.

"Yellow eyes saw us on the way. I don't trust him. He follows you like a puppy. Your mother's orders."

"Where to, then?" Feedaa questioned.

"Section four-seven." Sae Sae took the lead.

They took a right turn and then a left before reaching a small opening in the midst of a dense canopy. The sunlight that had seemed scalding after a few minutes in the open failed to light the path properly as they entered. The temperature dropped noticeably on the trail.

The dirt path ahead was narrow. Only one person could walk through it at a time.

Looking around, Sae Sae said, "We need to move in single file. Feedaa, you first, then Aayat. I will walk at the end."

Slowly they moved forward, dried leaves crunching under their shoes. Colourful flowers hung from trees and bushes growing on the sides, making the canopy vibrant despite the lack of light. Aayat touched a bush just to make sure she wasn't dreaming.

"It must have been even denser during your grand-mother's time," she said.

"Naah. From the old *Polaroid* I have seen, the jungle was in a pretty bad shape. Amji did a lot to bring it to this state." Feedaa smelled a flower.

"Really, why so? I mean I have always heard my grand-mother say that the planet was much greener in their time."

"It depends on how you treat the surroundings and exploit the resources," Sae Sae added from behind, his vigilant eyes looking in every direction to make sure no one followed them.

"Probably." Feedaa nodded in agreement. "Amji's parents ran a company that manufactured vehicles which ran on fossil fuels, the liquid you find in deposits under the river basins. Don't know what you call them."

"Petrol," Aayat replied.

"Yeah, maybe. We called them hydro-carbonaceous liquid. Anyways, so these vehicles released a lot of fumes and all. Amji says that there was a time they feared that the planet would collapse because of overheating. The temperatures soared, ice melted, and there was rain mixed with dangerous gases that burned people's skin."

"Acid rain," Aayat supplemented.

"Whatever. So people protested against the cars and other things that were releasing those exhausts. Amji was young. She hated that her parents were participants in making the planet worse. Therefore, she studied environmental science and took upon herself the responsibility to help restore the jungle. There are still several places outside Faejenda that suf-fer from the after-effects, but we are living a better life, thanks to Amji." Feedaa beamed with pride.

The path was getting narrower, and the canopy overhead hung lower with every step they took. The creepers inter-crossed and formed an arch above. Feedaa stooped to prevent herself from bumping into them. The coos of birds and chirping of the crickets became louder and clearer. Bees buzzed freely and the butterflies danced above the flowers. The fresh smell resembling that of eucalyptus became distinct at one point, making Aayat's heart beat fast from the familiarity.

"We need to drop down." Sae Sae held Aayat's shoulders and pushed her downwards.

"I think so, too. Aayat, we will have to crawl for a little while before we reach a clearing. Observe and follow." Feedaa crouched, almost lying flat on her stomach, and crawled on the path using her knees and elbows to push forward.

"Why didn't we go through the other one?" Aayat hated getting dirty. The track had turned muddy and was covered with a mix of fallen leaves, petals, and dead insects. Her stomach revolted at the thought of dipping her palms into that slick.

"First get down and move. We won't let you get hurt." Sae Sae's words of assurance surprised her.

As they edged forwards, he filled her in, "Aunt Errumm is the head of the district administration. She is busy most of the time and is constantly worried about Feedaa, and depends upon the staff to inform her of Feedaa's whereabouts."

"Well, given that she spends most of her time wandering around, any mother would be worried." Aayat inched a little further.

"You can't take her side," Feedaa shouted, crawling ahead of them.

"Then you should wear your lenses all the time, just like aunt asked you to," Sae Sae snapped from behind.

"Then she will know what we do at the lab, and *that*, my dear cousin, would prove to be very bad for your health." Feedaa stopped for a while, took deep breaths and resumed crawling forwards.

Though Aayat was worried about her pants getting stuck and torn, her skin getting bruised and her elbow getting scraped, the cousins continued banter kept her calm.

Soon they arrived in a clearing.

Scratched, sweaty, and tired, the three of them rose to their feet. The warm air that touched Aayat's skin felt welcoming. With parched throat and cracked lips, She looked around. In that vast expanse of strange territory filled with unknown fauna and flora, she found white Mayflowers hanging from the trees, which made her long for home. Suddenly a sharp pain shot through the middle of her chest and spread all over. She swallowed the boulder-sized lump lodged in her throat as tears threatened to lurk from the corner of her eyes.

Sniffling as quietly as possible, she concentrated on the surroundings. A random variety of smells—sweet, leafy, foul, and muddy, invaded her senses. Placing her foot on the spot that seemed like it would be the least noisy, Aayat asked, "How far to the stream?"

"About five hundred *senlon*," Sae Sae replied, brushing his clothes with his hands.

"*Senlon*?" Aayat squinted.

Feedaa placed her left and right foot at a specific distance apart and pointed. "One *senlon*."

"Aah." Aayat scratched her throat.

As if on cue, Sae Sae presented a water bottle from his bag.

"So your mother is the district magistrate?" Aayat gulped the water in a hurry, spilling a few drops on both sides of her mouth, and passed the bottle to Feedaa.

"What's that?" Feedaa threw a piece bark she'd torn from a tree trunk and grabbed the bottle.

"Ummm, one who runs the administration of the district?" Aayat wiped her mouth with the back of her hand.

"Oh, yeah, she is that." Feedaa smiled.

"And your father?"

"Don't know. Never met him."

"Sorry." Aayat looked at her shoes.

"That's fine. A lot of people ask about him," Feedaa replied, untangling the young, wild branches of trees and binding creepers properly around the trunks.

"So you use your mother's maiden name I suppose."

"Why would I use Mum's name when I have my own?" Feedaa was still busy sorting the creepers.

"I meant your last name, you know, family name. You and Sae Sae must share the . . . same . . ." Aayat's words trailed off as she saw the cousins looking at each other, Sae Sae furrowed his forehead and angry lines appeared at the corner of his lips.

"We don't have that here," he replied.

"What do we not have?" Feedaa turned to face Sae Sae

"We don't have second names or family names here. We recognise people by their own achievements and don't let them have a free ride based on their background."

Aayat pursed her lips. *This person never gives a straight reply. How am I supposed to know what they do or don't do in this world? When am I going to leave this place? God, please let me leave today. Please, let me flow through that stream and reach my world just like I reached this one.*

Mum must be worried. And my fish, oh poor fishy. Did anyone even feed it? It has been almost a week. There is going to be so much work piled up when I get back. What am I going to tell Dr. Ahuja? I ran away without giving notice—

"Aayat, Aayat." Feedaa shook her shoulders.

As if woken up from a trance she looked up. "Sorry, I was thinking about . . . never mind, what happened?"

"We are here. This is the spot where we found you." Sae Sae pointed at a spot near the freely flowing stream. Its clean water splashed downslope.

Aayat blinked her eyes. Her mind went blank.

Was it her way back?

Was it really her way back to the world she had known since childhood?

Was she finally going to return to her world and never look back?

Finally, she could have some rest.

Chapter Eight

The administration was planning a crackdown on street number 12.1, which was crawling with Djinns looking for ways to open a permanent portal to the human world. According to the information the administrative department received from the informants, the Djinns planned to start a ring wherein the criminals of the opposite world could be hired to commit a crime in the alternate world and then get sent back, leaving no chance for them to be caught.

They could not let that happen.

Errumm called her assistant and ordered her to arrange an emergency meeting. "I want to see everyone in the conference room in ten *twinks*, and not as holograms. I want every official present there in corporeal form."

A few moments later, walking towards the conference room, she tried contacting Feedaa. This was the ninth time that day that she could not get the authorisation for communication. Errumm dropped the call and sent a verbal message to the officials in the city asking if anyone had seen her daughter.

Yellow eyes responded within a few *twinks*, "She has gone towards the trail of Kausar with Sae Sae. I can go get them if you want."

Errumm thanked him and told him not to bother. She already had a meeting to attend and several dignitaries to please.

She is going to flunk her exams. And why is Sae Sae behaving so irresponsibly? Who goes hiking on a workday? Errumm muttered under her breath as her secretary opened the door for her.

Sixteen Djinns rose from their seats as Errumm entered. A teak coloured oval table with thick legs and the logo of the department embossed on the top stood in the middle of the conference hall, surrounded by thirty chairs. Illuminated by the white lights hidden underneath a false ceiling, the room had a bright yet serious undertone.

"Thank you, everyone, for assembling here on such short notice. I know you all are busy, but I wanted to meet so that all the departments can get to work as soon as possible," Errumm said, taking a seat. "I am sure you are familiar with street number twelve-one and the notorious elements occupying it. As discussed in the sun-cycle-beginning agenda, the administration wants to put them out of business for good."

A young aadjinn tried to speak. "Umm, well, I—" However, upon realizing that Errumm hadn't finished yet, his voice cut off.

"You have something to add?" She turned toward him—and so did all fifteen other department representatives sitting around the table.

"Yes, no, I mean yes. Well, I have something to say but, ummm, I will, after you have finished, madam." Beads of sweat formed on his forehead as he pursed his lips tightly, showing the dimples on his cheek.

"So, does anyone has any idea regarding how far we have advanced in the plan, or are we still in the waiting period?" Errumm returned to the discussion they were having before the interruption.

One of the senior officials who sat farthest away, wearing a black suit, replied, "We have sent some officials from the department to infiltrate them."

"And?" Errumm looked at him and then at the screen displaying his plan, which seemed incomplete. There were several blank spaces beside the dates.

"We are waiting for his signal."

"That's it? All you are doing is waiting? What about the Intel department? Are you waiting, too?" Errumm looked at other representatives.

The primly dressed aadjinn in a slate grey skirt suit representing the intel department spoke next. "We have placed heat-sensing and infra-red cameras to record the movements of everyone who goes in and leaves the street, and we also have bugs in place to record audio. A few of our officers have infiltrated the group, one of whom has climbed high up the ladder. Almost all information provided by that officer is correct, and she is now working on unearthing the origin of this obsession with the human world, to devise a permanent solution. Once we know how they found out about the portal, or whether they have any specific portal under their control, you know, around the street, we may be able to do a better job. We are also tracing their possible connections with the human world and how it began. We also—"

"Fine, I get the gist. Send the relevant files to my office. What else?" Errumm tapped her left foot.

The newly transferred representative of the Security Check department informed Errumm, "We are trailing their leader manually."

One of the officers sitting in the room asked, "Why manually?"

"To not miss out on anything. Despite hovering drone cameras with light-wave scanners, and heat and infra-red cameras, there are possibilities of blind spots. There are times when movements have been missed." The representative took a few sips of water before continuing, "You know the inhabitants of that part have put blockers and are also pretty good at dodging cameras, and they speak a different language among themselves. I am not sure if they devised it or if it's an ancient language. The officers trailing them have picked up a few words, and we are trying to reverse engineer the language."

"Do we have a concrete plan on how we will deal with these elements after all the information has been analysed?" Errumm cut in between.

Everyone looked right and left to avoid meeting her eyes. One of the bulbs flickered noisily as the room grew silent.

Errumm roared, "Seriously. Did I not make myself clear the last time we met? I do not want to hear any stupid updates. I want a *plan*, a concrete plan. Get all your heads together and give me one by the end of this moon cycle, or leave the post so that someone capable can fill in and get the work done."

No one stirred for several *twinks*.

"And you, the one who was so eager to cut me off. What did you have to say?"

The young aadjinn blinked his eyes, scratched the back of his neck absently, and willed his dry mouth to open. "I had a p—"

Errumm's secretary rushed inside before he could finish the sentence. "The chief commissioner is looking for you, madam administrator."

"I want to hear you. Go wait in my office. And the rest of you—I want a plan." Errumm banged her palms on the table before leaving the room.

Errumm's office was on the top floor of the building and was the largest in the department. It was a corner office with glass walls on two sides to allow her to monitor the activities of her subordinates. A large window on the brick wall opposite to the door opened on the outside. However, it was slammed shut when Tenzen arrived. He sat at the farthest edge of the green vinyl sofa, scratching his cuticles. He licked his dry lips and sipped water at regular intervals, keeping his focus on the door.

It took a long time for Errumm to return.

She motioned him to sit on a chair before her, across her office table. "Have a seat. What's your name?"

"Tenzen," the young officer said as he got up from the sofa and took a seat opposite Errumm.

"Yes, Tenzen, what was so important?"

His face had shrunk in the time he spent waiting and his lips were scorched. He took deep breaths before speaking. "I have a plan. We can eliminate the entire mess of these human-loving Djinns once and for all."

Errumm leaned closer and narrowed her eyes. The young aadjinn had been successful in getting her attention.

Aayat stood at the bank of the stream looking at the water without blinking. Everything had come to a halt—her mind had become a blank canvas.

"What do we do now?" Feedaa asked, standing beside Aayat.

Sae Sae kept quiet for a while. He then marked the place where they'd found Aayat with an X using a stone lying nearby. "The stream comes from up there," he said, pointing towards the hill range to the east of the valley. "I think she must have been walking around that area and probably fell downhill." He looked at Aayat, but she stared back without any response.

Nothing that was going on made any sense to her. If it was a dream, it was a terrifyingly long one, and if it wasn't, then she was way beyond her depth. Earlier, she's thought once they reached the stream, she'd know what to do or where the starting point of the fiasco was and a solution would come to her miraculously, but now she understood that nothing she'd been hoping for was going to happen.

The bright sunny day darkened in an instant. Voices became distant and her legs turned liquid.

"Aayat, Aayat." Feedaa held her by the shoulders and said, "Breathe, take deep breaths, deep breaths."

A blurry figure began forming in front of Aayat's eyes—a tall young female with a robotic voice.

"Breathe." A stony cold and dry robotic voice ordered.

She gulped. A gush of warm air filled her lungs. Her vision became clear. Feedaa rubbed her frigid, cold palms, taking one at a time between her large, warm ones.

She blinked her eyes, and tears streamed downwards. Sae Sae's frown-lined face turned blurry.

"Are you all right?" Feedaa shook her shoulders.

"Yes."

"Here, have some *rokoto*." Sae Sae offered her a magenta-coloured beverage from a thermos flask. Aayat drank it in a hurry and coughed. Her brain failed to register the taste.

He scoffed. "You can't even drink it right."

Beads of sweat streamed down Aayat's temples and flowed past the sides of her cheeks.

"Let's walk upstream," Feedaa suggested, helping Aayat up on her feet.

Aayat tried to stand, but slumped. Feedaa held her tightly and helped her stand again. She gave her some water, then waited for a while, letting her take several deep breaths.

The trio walked in silence.

After what felt like an eternity, Sae Sae asked, "You wearing covers?"

Feedaa shook her head.

"What's covers?" Aayat asked, more to divert her attention than out of curiosity.

"It's, umm, like a high ended gadget that slides on the surface of your eyes." Feedaa explained, sliding her right hand over her eyes.

"Aah, contact lens. The ones used for correcting vision." Aayat nodded absently.

"No not for vision. It's for—how to explain? What gadget do you use to surf for information, send and receive communication, watch over the children, project pictures and videos on screen, and other such things?" Feedaa blurted out the functions of the cover in a single breath.

"It does all of that?" Aayat raised her eyebrows.

"Yeah." Feedaa's expression failed to mask the pride she felt for their advanced technology.

"And you just wear it in your eye?"

"Yes." Feedaa squinted.

"So why are you not wearing it then?" Aayat asked, using their conversation as an excuse to push the thought of her future out of her mind at least for the time being. They would return to haunt her once she would be alone in the lab.

"My mother keeps an eye on me using the covers. She had somehow got my covers altered so I can't turn off my location, and she keeps tracking it."

"Why does she keep an eye on you?"

"Well, she is the head of the district administration who offends people sometimes. Actually, she offends people all the time. She thinks those people might harm me for revenge." Feedaa plunged an imaginary knife into her chest.

Aayat smiled at her answer. "Mother's love. I guess it's the same all over the universe, probably in the entire galaxy or the other galaxies inhabited by intelligent beings."

They kept walking further, gossiping, exchanging details about their worlds and families.

Feedaa elbowed Aayat and questioned, "What about your family?"

"My father is a doctor, an oncologist. And my mother is a climatologist. They live in another town, about a thousand kilometres from here."

"Near the sea?" Feedaa sounded quite sure, as if she knew what existed where in Aayat's world.

"Yeah. You have a sea in the east here, too?" Any sense of familiarity felt like a hug from an old lover—comfortable and warm, like pieces fitting in together.

"I told you, physical features are the same." Sae Sae snapped a twig to make way. "Now, stop chit-chatting and concentrate on the surroundings. Do you recognise anything? The place where you fell or got lost in your world? Anything that looks like it could be a door to your world?"

"Why do you always have to be this strict? She is trying, give her some space." Feedaa turned a little in his direction and rolled her eyes.

"And all you know is how to waste time," he replied, pointing towards a non-existent clock in the air.

Feedaa shrugged her shoulders and turned towards Aayat. "Do you remember anything? Anything at all?" she asked softly.

Aayat closed her eyes tight and recalled the day in question. She could see herself walking on the sides of the road, past a *caution* sign, the down slope towards the dirt road, the rustling of leaves, the descending sun, the cold drizzle, and then nothing. A complete blank. She opened her eyes and shut them again, desperate to fill that blank. Her heart drummed against the rib cage and her legs trembled. The blank was still blank.

"You don't remember anything," Feedaa said, dejectedly answering the question swirling in the mind of all three.

"Can we please sit for a while?" Aayat felt tired, weighed down by the expectations of all three of them.

"Sure." Feedaa came to a halt instantly.

They sat on the wild tuft of grass and weed growing along the shore of the stream. Breezes tousled by the waves caressed their faces.

Alien land, alien people, alien ways of life.

Aayat brought her knees to her chest and hugged herself, shrinking away from the cousins. Her stomach felt leaden. She buried her face in her knees and willed the darkness to swallow her.

Intermittent coos of birds and howls of animals were the only thing piercing the quiet—until Sae Sae's communication device blared.

"Aunt Errumm," he shouted. Aayat raised her head and rubbed her eyes to bring them to focus.

"Hurry, find a spot far away from here," Feedaa urged her, jumping into action.

He ran in the opposite direction. Aayat could see the back of Errumm's form that materialized in thin air. She sat on a leather chair and roared loudly. Feedaa stood beside Aayat and observed the scene from afar. From the corner of her eyes, Aayat saw Feedaa's lips twitch as her cousin and her mother discussed her whereabouts.

Sae Sae returned, his ears red with anger. "You are going to get both of us killed one day."

"Shall we head back?"

"What else is left to do?" Sae Sae didn't sound angry. His voice was emotionless.

"Don't worry, we will find a way," Feedaa rested her hand on his shoulders. "Not only to send Aayat back, but also to get uncle back."

Chapter Nine

Aayat twisted the scarf in her hands absently, sitting on the floor. She had slumped there as soon as they entered the study, not bothering to find a chair. Feedaa stared at her, sitting cross-legged in front of her, and Sae Sae sulked in a distant corner.

"What time is it?" Sae Sae broke the silence.

"Close to seven *rahep*," Feedaa replied.

"You must get going." Sae Sae spoke without looking at Feedaa.

"What's *rahep*?"

Aayat looked at Feedaa, who thought for a while before answering, "Unit of time. Will explain the detail later."

She then went to the adjoining chamber, which served as a makeshift kitchen, and brought the food she'd asked her mother to prepare for Sae Sae. Placing it on the wooden table in the centre of the study she asked the other two to join. "You need energy to work, so eat first and think later."

Sae Sae reluctantly dragged two chairs for himself and Feedaa and left Aayat on her spot. He did not know what to say to her, so he let her be until Feedaa pulled her up and brought her to the table and thrust a chicken wrap in her hand.

They were nibbling through the food when Feedaa jumped from her seat, exclaiming, "Damn, damn, damn."

"What now?" Sae Sae glared at her.

"Check the security footage! Ray is here, and she is coming in. Sae Sae, she is coming in—do something, do something."

She pointed at the screen on the left corner of the wall behind Sae Sae. It played continuous feed from the security cameras, to let Sae Sae know what went on in the bunker while he was cooped up in the study.

Sae Sae leapt out of the study at his cousin's words. Feedaa and Aayat aligned their chairs in front of the screen displaying the security footage to observe the conversation between Ray and him.

"Hey honey, what are you doing here so late?" he asked, looking at Ray as if she had risen form dead. They stood face to face in the room Aayat had been occupying for the last few days.

"I got here way late. Anyhow there is something I need to tell you." Ray kept walking towards the study.

"Why don't we talk here? It's stuffy inside." Sae Sae cleared his throat and approached her in a sprint like manner, his hands in his pant pockets.

"What's wrong with you? Why are you behaving like this?" Ray squinted.

"Well, uh, let's go out and eat." He shrugged.

"Is everything all right? You seem strange. Are you sick or something? I said I need to discuss something very important, and you want to go out?" Ray touched his cheek lightly. Her red flared skirt fluttered a little as she turned to reach his cheek. Her short frame seemed mousy to Aayat in comparison to Feedaa's broad one. The two audjinns seemed poles apart. Ray had a sad predisposition. Her light brown almond shaped eyes didn't smile, even if her thin pink lips did.

"Fine then, just tell me already." Sae Sae removed her hand and led her towards the black vinyl couch near the window Aayat was unable to open.

Ray looked at him closely, narrowing her eyes, and blinked twice before speaking. "I met someone a few nights back. They said they knew a lot about the portal, you know, details, like how to find those people and all."

Feedaa and Aayat looked at one another in wild anticipation, and turned towards the screen again.

"So?" Sae Sae's mild tone astonished Aayat. She expected him to jump in anger at the mention of *those people*.

"I know you don't like other people interfering in your business, but they can help." Ray came closer, kept her hand on Sae Sae's knees and whispered, "Let me look at your father's journals. Maybe there is something that corroborates their words." The bug in her ear allowed Aayat to listen to the inaudible whisper. They were somehow connected on the audio interface.

Sae Sae exhaled and said, "How many times have I told you not to listen to any crap that those people feed you? They'll say anything to get you to trust them and lay hands on my father's work. If there was a way listed in his research notes, we would have found it by now." He almost threw her hand off his knees.

"What's the harm in looking?" Ray stood up and took a few steps toward the study.

Sae Sae stood up, looked at his feet, shifted his weight from left to right foot, rubbed the nape of his neck and then spoke calmly. "Ray, let's take a break."

"We haven't even started working," she replied with her back towards him.

"Not from work. From us."

The words stopped Ray on the spot. She turned, lifted her head slowly to look at him and opened her eyes and mouth wide but did not say anything.

"We, us, you and me, I mean, we both are exhausted. You have your job and family and I have this, ummm . . . you know. I need to get a job, a serious job and there is an experiment, I was, uhhh, thinking of completing my studies . . ." Sae Sae seemed to be saying whatever came to his mind.

Feedaa squeezed Aayat's hand as both crept closer to the screen. Their heads were hardly an inch away from it.

"Stop talking, Sae Sae. Just *stop talking*."

"Yes, Ma'am." Sae Sae slapped his hands on his side and stood in attention.

Feedaa laughed and clapped her hands.

"And what exactly does this *break* entail?" Ray's heels click-clacked as she walked towards Sae Sae.

"I-It-I think it came out wrong. I meant, why don't we take a break from all the search work and all. It's exhausting, and we have a life to look forward to . . ."

"You, *you* of all people want us to stop searching? At least say something believable, Sae Sae." Ray almost reached his collar but then brought her hands back to her sides and balled them into a fist. She took a last look at him and stomped out of the lab.

The night sky was cool, and the stars twinkled brightly, yet all Ray could see was a narrow, dark path leading towards an endless tunnel. She took off her heels and walked barefoot to absorb the cool of the metal road beneath her soles. A strange uneven mix of anger, pity, remorse, pain, and longing clouded her being.

Someone requested an audience through her communication device. Her first impulse was to reject the request, but then she authorized the connection.

"Ray, did you get the papers?" the voice on the other side asked.

"Stop calling me and stop talking to me. I am out," she snapped.

"So you didn't get the papers?" the person on the other side said with an obvious smirk.

"I don't *want* to get them. It is *my* choice to not give you the information. If you want something, go to administrator Errumm and get a signed order. Stop involving me in your games and stop coming to my house." She felt like throwing the device at his face, but they weren't talking face-to-face so she disconnected the call and switched off the device.

Not wanting to go home, she walked towards the jungle. The trail of Kausar was near. It was where she had first realised that Sae Sae was the only one in the world who believed her. Everyone else told her to shut up as soon as she told them about her little sister, Amber, but not him. He'd spent countless hours with her, walking through the winding paths, marking the trees, and scratching the stones for answers. He believed in her, and that was what made her fall for him. He believed it because she said it and that was enough for her to love him.

They had spent so many *raheps* relishing the colours of fresh blooming flowers and the smell of rain-drenched soil. It was near the oldest tree on the trail that Sae Sae had confessed his love for her, on a moonless, dark night in the midst of the wilderness, and that, too, without any befitting gift, then apologised for doing so. But she loved his spontaneity. The way he did everything without notice made her heart race.

Maybe he just blurted it out without thinking. Maybe he was busy, and I disturbed him. Maybe he just got angry at the thought of having to share his father's journals. I shouldn't have listened to those people. I'll talk to him after a few days. His anger may have subsided by then.

A moon cycle ago, an anonymous caller had contacted her. He told her that the administration was planning to round up everyone who was pro-human or worked to find ways to pass through the interregnum. They promised to keep Sae Sae out of trouble if Ray would give them his father's notes. Scared for her fiancé, she had agreed to help them. Hardly did she know that it would blow up in her face.

Sae Sae entered the study with heavy steps and, as soon as he saw Feedaa, roared, "Lose the grin."

"I am not grinning." Feedaa tried to bring her lips back into position. They had spread from ear to ear, making it very difficult to mask her happiness about the breakup.

She stretched diagonally on a rug spread near the bookrack, yawned loudly and said, "Oh, I am so tired. This entire trail and stream business was such a bust. Anyhow, all is well that ends well."

Sae Sae looked at her with the eyes of a hunting hound, ready to lash out. Were Aayat not there, he might have started a fistfight with his cousin already. However, he simply kicked Feedaa's shoes, sending them flying to the far corner of the room. He couldn't help shouting, "What ended well?"

"You know." Feedaa yawned again and continued, "That stupid business you had with that Ray. I am glad it ended, and I am sure mum will be glad, too."

"Get out. Go Home. Your mother will blame me if you fail the exams," Sae Sae said, opening the door of the study.

"I am so sorry. It all happened because of me. I am really sorry. I know I can't talk to your fiancée to convince her, but I'll do anything else you want to help convince her." Aayat spoke in a small voice. She was still seated near the screen.

Feedaa said absently, "Don't be. It's good riddance anyway. I'd rather he dated you."

"Feedaa," Sae Sae shouted. "Don't just say anything that comes to your mind. Get a filter."

"Why not? She is intelligent, crafty, witty, a scientist, and pretty, too. I like her." Feedaa winked.

"You think this is some fantasy ride? Why would I like her? She is so clum—" Sae Sae broke off as he remembered Aayat was in the same room. He looked at her sheepishly, but she was smiling. He scoffed, and soon the three of them were laughing.

"Let's have some of your *rokoto,* Sae Sae." Feedaa went to Aayat, stood behind her, and whispered in her ears, "Were you offended? I hope not. I hate people who take offense easily. They are such *Keefe.*"

"Waste of a person?" Aayat's lips curved upwards in a smile.

"Wow, you are one fast learner, Aayat. I like you so much more than Ray. It would be really great if that dim-witted Sae Sae could date you. But you are too smart for him."

"Let's cut that joke." Aayat made a cross with her hands.

"Why? You don't like my cousin?"

"I thought it was a joke." Aayat widened her eyes.

"It was, but—"

"Cut it out, Feedaa. Know when to snap out of something." Sae Sae came back with three mugs and a tumbler full of *rokoto.* He poured the magenta-coloured aromatic liquid and slid the cup towards the two females of different species who came to the table and sat in front of him.

"This is delicious," Aayat exclaimed, taking a sip from the cup.

"Don't you have it in your world?" Feedaa asked in a quirky voice.

"No."

"Then what?" Feedaa licked the last drop of *rokoto* and banged the cup on the table.

"Tea, coffee. They are made of plant leaves and berries—mostly dark brown or blackish. People drink it according to taste—with milk, without milk, with sugar, without sugar."

"I want to taste it," Feedaa piped.

"Yeah, me, too. Abee wrote at length about the food in your world." Sae Sae picked his cup and nodded, looking at the wooden rack filled with his father's journals.

"We know very little about each other. Let's play your

truth and mine," Feedaa suggested, straightening on the chair.

"What's that?" Aayat removed a tendril of hair from her face.

"It's like we will share secrets that no one else in the world knows and that will—"

"Why would she play such a childish game?" Sae Sae interrupted.

"Why wouldn't she? Not everyone is a buzz kill like you." Feedaa stuck her tongue out.

"I am out then," he said, getting up to leave—when Feedaa's communication device buzzed.

"Mum! It's mum, oh my God, it's mum." She jumped from her seat and looked from the device on her wrist to Sae Sae, to Aayat, to the device again.

"Stop jumping around like that, and authorise the communication," Sae Sae said, more irritated than alarmed.

"How? Aayat, she will see Aayat." Feedaa was still jumping.

"Move to the other room then, hurry," Sae Sae said, signalling her to go outside the study.

"Hey mum, I was just about to come home," Feedaa began as a life-sized hologram of Errumm, sitting on a chair, materialised in the lab. Sae Sae could see the back of her head, the sides of her hands as they were resting on the arms of the chair, and the heels of her shoes. Even from this angle, she looked crisp, as if ready to appear on a nationwide broadcast.

"And when exactly were you planning on doing that?" the hologram asked in a stern voice.

"Woooo, Mum."

"Where is Sae Sae?" the hologram questioned.

"Right here, let me call him," Feedaa flicked her hand, gesturing Sae Sae to join the conversation.

"And where is the third wheel? The one both of you have

been roaming all around the town with?"

Sae Sae stopped dead on his tracks as he heard Errumm's hologram ask for Aayat. In a fit of nervousness, Feedaa disconnected the communication.

"Why did you disconnect it? Now Aunt Errumm is going to raise hell." Sae Sae's forehead crowded with frowns.

"What was I supposed to do, then?"

Aayat came running in.

"How did she know about me?" Aayat asked, looking at them in turns.

"Did you hear the conversation?" Sae Sae enquired.

"Yes, now think, how on earth did she know about me?" Aayat repeated the question.

"Yellow eyes," Feedaa and Sae Sae cried in unison.

"What are we going to do now?" Feedaa turned towards Sae Sae, looking like a lost little puppy.

"It's okay. Relax. Breathe. Let me come with you. I will talk to aunt, it's not your fault, you have nothing to worry about. I am here, I'll take care of things." Sae Sae held Feedaa's hands.

Aayat stepped forward. "No. I will talk to her. It's all on me."

"*No*. My mother is the head of the district administration planning a siege on Djinn who love humans. You think talking to her is the best idea?"

"Do you have a better one, then?" Aayat raised her eyebrows. "Let's go there. Take me with you and I will talk to your mother. Trust me. Whatever it is, we have to visit her. It's better that she knows." Aayat ran her hand over her pants and smoothed her hair.

Sae Sae looked at Aayat, on board with the idea. "What are we going to tell her?"

"The truth. That I wandered off in the jungle, slipped into the stream, and ended up in your world. You brought me here to save me from dying and it is not your fault that I don't know how I came here or how to return to my world."

"What do you think will happen then? Mum is going to order to have you taken you into custody, and they are going to interrogate you like a runaway criminal and you will be stuck here forever," Feedaa said, her voice wavering.

"She is right. Let's go to your house together," Sae Sae spoke, still holding Feedaa's hand. "Why don't you go fasten the piece of cloth around your head, and I'll get the car." He patted Feedaa's shoulder and went outside as Aayat rushed to get the scarf.

CHAPTER TEN

A jammer at Errumm's house blocked the functions of all the unauthorized devices and software programs and made it the safest place to discuss confidential matters.

Tenzen sat in the living room, anticipating her questions, playing imaginary scenarios in his head, as she emerged from the kitchen. Placing a cup of *rokoto* in front of him, she asked, "Are you sure that your aadjinn will not sell us out?"

"Audjinn, and she is a very trusted colleague. She will never betray us." He replied slowly, taking time with each word. "She is quite close with the second-in-command of the group, has a good network, and has almost always helped me." He looked at Errumm expectantly, biting his lips, awaiting her reaction.

"People are not as simple as you think, newbie. There is a lot you need to learn." Errumm fiddled with the micro-chip sticking to her wrist and crossed her legs.

"I know. I have had quite an interesting childhood," he replied, laughing nervously. He then shifted a bit closer and spoke in a hushed tone. "May I ask you something, ma'am? If you don't mind."

"What?" Errumm raised her head.

"Your husband, I mean ex-husband, was a human supporter?"

"Hmmm," Errumm grunted in response.

Tenzen wanted to ask something else, too, but the question died in his throat at the sight of his superior's twitching lip. Although she looked charismatic in a beige top over navy blue track pants, her demeanour never let him forget her position in the outside world.

"Is that all, or do you want to confirm any other rumour?"

"No ma'am. Thank you so much. I would like to take my leave for the day."

Tenzen got up and walked towards the door as Errumm kept sitting on the chair, looking at oblivion. On his way out he saw Errumm's daughter, her cousin—and a strange audjinn with a piece of cloth wrapped around her head.

Aayat, Feedaa, and Sae Sae stood close to the entrance of the living room, their hands tied to the front and eyes glued to the floor as Errumm hovered over. She had stopped them before they could walk any further and sit.

"Look at me," she roared, hands on her hip.

Feedaa and Sae Sae raised their eyes obediently. Aayat looked sideways, unable to face Errumm's authoritative figure.

One of the walls of the room was made of thick transparent glass and overlooked the garden. She caught sight of the bright purple flowers resembling petunias in the flower beds and thought of her mother, how she tended to their garden as her father had immersed himself in finding cures for his patients. Every visitor complimented her mother for such a well-kept garden. If they only knew what pain it hid.

"Who do you think you two are?" Errumm's voice brought Aayat back to the present. She raised her eyelids and observed how different Errumm looked form her daughter at the moment—a stern face, upright posture with broad shoulders and jet black eyes, although both were equally tall.

"Mum, let's calm down."

"Aunt Errumm, please just listen."

Both voices were small and timid. Even Sae Sae's ferocious

stance was subdued.

Errumm brought her wrist closer and mumbled some instructions into the chip attached to it. The glass walls turned opaque, lights turned milder, and white noise jutted in.

"Nothing that happens in this room can be traced, tracked, or recorded. So, *you* tell me why you are here and what do you want." Errumm turned towards Aayat, whose mouth dried instantly.

"Mum, you need to relax." Feedaa came closer and held her mother's hand, but Errumm jerked her aside.

"Speak."

"Aunt, let's sit and talk. Shall we?" Sae Sae took small steps toward the white sofa in the middle of the room. Feedaa followed close behind, dragging Aayat along with her.

"Sure." Errumm took a seat opposite Aayat on the chair fitted with white furry cushion and crossed her hands on her chest. Her piercing gaze landed on Aayat's face, which turned red. The room became hotter as sweat dripped down Aayat's temple under the scarf, and the hair at the back of her neck stood upright.

She cleared her throat and spoke, "Hello ma'am, I am Aayat Athar."

"What?" Errumm squinted.

"Oh, I forgot. Mum, you need to wear these ear pods to talk to her or you won't understand what she is saying." Feedaa produced a plastic case from her pocket and opened it. The ear pods lay listlessly.

"What's this now?" Errumm looked at Sae Sae for answer.

"Abee devised these, to help us communicate with the humans. They speak a different language."

"Your father was a great inventor." Errumm picked up the pods and placed them inside her ears. Feedaa jumped to help but when her mother glowered at her, she leapt back to her seat.

Errumm turned to Aayat and pointed her long, cylindrical fingers at the scarf. "Remove that thing from your face and head, first. It's distracting."

Aayat followed the command. The lush black hair spilled freely across her shoulders.

Errumm turned her head in Sae Sae's direction in the meanwhile and spoke through her teeth, saying, "I knew you would do something like this one day. Sae Sae, I warned you not to behave irresponsibly. Not only did you bring a human to your lab, but also you involved my daughter in your shenanigans."

"Mum, you cannot talk to him like that. This is not fair. You don't even know the whole story and you start blaming us. This is not the Administrative block."

"Feedaa, stop it," Sae Sae intervened. "I know, Aunt. I am sorry it came to this. I really didn't mean for any of it to happen, but we couldn't leave a living being in the middle of the jungle to become animal fodder."

"So you brought her home." Errumm banged her palms on the table. Aayat felt the need to close her ears to avoid hearing Errumm's thunderous voice.

Feedaa glared at her mother. "What else were we supposed to do?"

"Hand her over to the administration."

"And then? Let her rot in that building-without-a-window forever?"

Aayat saw Sae Sae squeeze Feedaa's hand under the table as she argued with her mother.

"We would have found a way out. Things need to happen systematically, Feedaa. *You cannot defy the law*," Errumm screamed.

"Yeah, and what has your *law* given me? A father-less existence?"

Aayat gasped at Feedaa's words as Errumm opened her

mouth and closed it again. Sae Sae sat exceptionally still, looking at Feedaa without blinking. For several seconds, everyone stayed silent. Something ticked continuously in the background, filling the void.

Not knowing what else to do, Aayat spoke, "Ma'am, it is not their fault. Please give me a chance to explain," she said as she licked her lips. "One evening I was walking through the jungle and slipped into the stream, and the next time I opened my eyes, I was in Sae Sae's lab. None of us knew what to do. We were all scared and clueless, and they were trying to protect me. It's not their fault. I am sorry for all of this." She looked at Errumm for a split second and then looked away, fixing her gaze on her shoes, waiting for the audjinn to say something awful.

Errumm looked at her and said, "Those are my clothes that you are wearing."

"Sorry, ma'am."

Errumm scoffed. "I knew these kids were going to do something like this someday." She then turned towards her daughter and mouthed something noiselessly. Her lips moved, but Aayat couldn't hear a thing.

Aayat pursed her lips and wiped her temples with her wrist. She then stole a quick glance at them and crept to the opposite corner of the living room, leaving the other three to resolve their issues.

A life-size dark brown sculpture of a barren tree stood in the far right corner of the room. It felt rough to her touch, as if she were really touching the bark. Several leafless branches protruded out of it. The room was devoid of any other artifact. It was carpeted end to end and seemed opposite to the overly decorated living room of her house—no pictures, no paintings, no vase at every corner, no designer wall papers. Aayat observed the spotless shiny walls, trying to figure out the material with which they were painted or wall-papered, scratching the cuticles of her index finger with her thumb. Now that Errumm was not in her vicinity, the room temperature seemed to have returned to normal. She wasn't perspiring profusely.

"Stop doing that. It's a bad habit," Errumm chided. "Tell me why you are here?" She had crossed over the room without Aayat realizing.

Aayat backed a little, putting some more distance between them. "I-I don't know. I didn't intend to come here. I had no idea a world like this even existed."

Errumm laughed exactly as Sae Sae did. "And you call yourself a scientist?"

Aayat blinked.

"What scientist doesn't believe in the existence of an alternate world?" Errumm brought her face closer to Aayat's in a dramatic manner and pulled away. She then spoke instructions to the chip on her wrist, and two cushioned wrought iron seats unfolded from the walls close to where they stood. Aayat jumped as one of them touched her legs but regained control soon.

"Oh . . . I had read about it, but a lot of things seem like speculation until you encounter them." Aayat took a seat beside Errumm, chewed her lower lip for a while, waiting for Errumm's sarcasm to take over, but when none came, she continued, "If you don't mind me asking, how did you know about me?"

"Yellow eyes reported it."

Aayat smiled slightly at the mention.

"What?" Errumm straightened.

"Nothing." She shook her head and looked at Errumm, whose angry eyes forced her to spill the beans, "It's just that Feedaa knows you spy on her." She tried hard not to smile again.

"You think I am scared of her knowing that? I'm her

mother. I have the right to know where she is, what she is doing." Errumm waved her hand in every direction just like Feedaa.

Despite not wanting to, Aayat laughed.

"What now?" Errumm paused and looked at her.

"Nothing," Aayat closed her mouth and pursed her lips, trying to kill the laugh in her throat.

"You always keep laughing and smiling at nothing?" Errumm stiffened.

"No, ma'am." Aayat made a poker face, trying not to offend her any further.

"Then?"

"You look exactly like Feedaa right now," she said meekly.

"Oh." Errumm looked sideways and smiled.

Feedaa and Sae Sae came to them in the meanwhile. Upon Feedaa's instructions, two more chairs unfolded beside Errumm's.

"What did you tell yellow eyes about her?" Errumm asked as they took their seats.

"Nothing specific. We told him that we were with a friend from down south," Sae Sae explained, placing a hand on his right knee.

"And what if he had asked for identification or something like that?" Errumm questioned.

"You remember my mother's friend whose house caught fire some time back? She and her husband were burnt down with all their belongings."

"Yes, I know. What a rotten thing to happen," Errumm said as she nodded her head.

"They had a daughter, Zenzee."

"But she died before her parents. When she was nineteen." Errumm looked at Sae Sae.

"Yes, but they never registered her death. Somehow they could never bring themselves to go to the authorities to tell them that their only child was dead," Sae Sae explained further.

"So you planned to introduce this human as Zenzee?" Errumm frowned at them.

Feedaa filled her mother in, "Yes, and we would have told him that her identification burnt down in the fire and that she was too depressed to go to get another one and had lost her ability to speak."

"And what would you have done had he asked for a biometric check?"

"Well he didn't." Feedaa clicked her tongue. "And that's that."

"You and your elaborate lies. Is this how you deceive me, too?" Errumm cocked her head and looked at her daughter.

Feedaa laughed and muttered in Aayat's ears, "See this is why she is still single." And then she turned to her mother suddenly. "By the way, Mum," she said, bringing her mouth dramatically closer to Errumm, "who was the aadjinn we saw leaving the house?"

"Who?"

"The one in navy blue pin-striped formal wear, yay high." Feedaa raised her hands to define Tenzen's height, "Slightly chubby cheeks."

"Oh, Tenzen, he is a new appointee at the administrative department."

"Anything else that I must know?" Feedaa imitated her mother's stern manner of questioning.

"Like what?"

"Like, should I expect any engagement announce—"

"Feedaa, when will you learn to keep your thoughts to yourself?" Errumm smacked the back of her daughter's head. Her face turned red. She looked at Aayat and then looked away quickly.

"Let's eat something." Sae Sae got up.

"I'll help prepare." Feedaa jumped up and dashed after Sae Sae.

Left alone with Errumm, Aayat fished for a topic. She looked around and then cleared her throat and said, "I thought you people would have robots to do the menial chores."

"Sorry?" Errumm's forehead was lined with wrinkles. She seemed to have not heard Aayat's words.

"Robots. I don't know what you call them here. Machines programmed to mimic human actions or assist them." Then she remembered that she was in an alternate universe and added hurriedly, "Of course, in your case they would mimic Djinn actions."

Errumm thought for a while, "Do you mean the Djinn Imitation Hardware?"

"What?"

"They are programmed to imitate our actions and perform them in cases where we are not able to or do not want to."

"Yeah, something like that." Aayat nodded and looked around, expecting one to come out any minute. There was only one door in the room and opened into the lawn. The opposite wall had a huge arch that led to the corridor connecting the living room to the rest of the house.

"We do not have one here." Errumm scratched her chin.

"Why not?" It seemed strange that a world so dependent upon computer programs, markedly advanced compared to her world, didn't have robots.

"We had them when I was small, around forty sun cycles back, but there were debates and conferences, and protests against its use and it was decided that having extremely intelligent DIH will ultimately make us handicapped so the government banned their use."

"DIH?"

"Djinn Imitation Hardware," Errumm replied, rolling her

eyes.

"But you have these chips and holograms and all."

Errumm sighed, looking irritated, and replied, "That's different. They aid our jobs and help in communication, but do not make independent decisions. We are the ones who decide."

Aayat had several follow-up questions, but felt as if staying quiet suited the mood more.

Feedaa definitely takes after her father. How does Errumm live with herself? Madam high and mighty. It's so suffocating, sitting in front of her like this. Doesn't even know how to treat a guest.

To Aayat's relief, Sae announced dinner through his chip, bringing an end to the conversation.

Feedaa took Aayat and the food to her room. Errumm let the younger audjinn have her way as she had other things to discuss with Sae Sae.

"What are you planning to do now?" Errumm asked Sae Sae over dinner as she put food on Sae Sae's plate. They were seated in the cosy dining room with a black wrought-iron four-seater dining table in the centre. The wall between the dining room and the kitchen was removed so it looked like an extension of the kitchen. A huge chandelier hung over the table which was laden with food—spiced meat, spinach bread, blanched goose, and a tumbler of *rokoto*, Sae Sae's favourite drink.

"We went to the stream hoping she might remember something, anything that could lead us to the portal, interregnum, or at least a hint of how to reach there, but it was all useless. And I can't blame her. If it were that easy, Abee would have returned ages ago," Sae Sae said, playing with the food on his plate.

"So, what's the next step?" Errumm pierced a piece of meat with her fork and lead it to her mouth.

"There has to be something that links the two of them. Aayat and Abee. I will find that link."

"How?"

Sae Sae stuffed his mouth and chewed for a while before answering. "I think there has to be a reason the portal opened for these two. I mean I have been there several times, no, thousands of times. I have been to those woods in the morning, late at night, during the daytime, in the evening, and all seasons. I never saw an opening. Why did it open for them and not for me? Or maybe there is another condition that I can't place my hands on now. There has to be some connection. It can't be a random coincidence. Now that I have three cases, Abee's, Amber's, and Aayat's, I can compare them against one another to identify the similarities and dissimilarities, and go on from there."

Errumm smiled at him lovingly. "You were always so smart. Why did you leave your studies midway? You can be anything you want. I will help you out. Start afresh, Sae Sae. There is nothing in the world that would make us all happier than seeing you succeed, my child." He was an exact copy of her brother—both in looks and temperament. It broke her heart to see him in the disheveled, broken state he was in at the moment.

"I am happy. Don't worry about me. Feedaa is already a handful." Sae Sae took another bite and chewed noisily.

"Well, there is something you should know," Errumm said, coming closer, her forehead crowded with wrinkles as she spoke. "Our department is planning a crackdown by the end of the next moon cycle. You need to find a way out before that. You really really need to send this human away. I won't be able to help you if she gets caught. So please, whatever you do, just hurry up. And if you cannot do anything, at least look for a way to send her out of the province by then. The eastern provinces haven't yet agreed to the siege. They might not participate in it. I can help you get her there."

Sae Sae nodded and stared at his plate, his mind fast-forwarding through the action plan. Thirty-eight days were all they were left with.

Chapter Eleven

Sae Sae and Aayat sat in the study around the central table, pouring over the research papers and journals. All window screens were up. A bright stream of light filled the room, filtered through the tinted glass. Even the hay-coloured walls looked cheerful. Aayat's hair was tied in a neat ponytail, and she wore Sae Sae's navy light blue t-shirt over burgundy track pants, which hung loosely on her body but felt comfortable, as compared to Errumm's crisp ones. She listened to the audio file while Sae Sae browsed through the written material. He had on an orange jumpsuit, which surprised Aayat. In contrast to his general apparent indifference, the colour was quite vibrant.

Outside the lab, through the window, trees dotted the landscape as far as Aayat could see, her only connection to the outside world.

"Concentrate, Aayat, we have very little time left." Sae Sae's expressions were mild. His eyes weren't the usual ball of anger, and there were hardly any frowns on his face. He had somehow softened since their visit to Errumm's place the previous night.

"Yeah, sorry. It just looked nice," she said, running her hand through her hair.

"We can go for a stroll later if you want."

Why is he being so nice? Like I am some sacrificial lamb.

"Fine, walk me through the plan." She folded her hands on her chest and rested her back on the chair.

"We have until the next full moon to work on your escape,"

he said, as he wrote something on the digital pad.

It was all gibberish to Aayat—the script, the calendar.

"What's that?" she asked.

"We have thirty-seven days—till the next full moon," he explained.

"Why are you people still stuck in lunar and solar calendars?" Aayat raised her eyebrows.

"Because we never met you. Now, can we focus?" Sae Sae shrugged his shoulders.

"I am listening." She looked at the aadjinn sitting in front of her.

"This is what we need to do—find the details about the night you came here, or Abee went there, and then compare the details of both cases to look for similarities. There has to be a trigger to your travel between the two dimensions. Something that connects these disappearances—day, date, month or any occurrence common on all days of travels through the portal."

"Those might be a coincidence," Aayat said, placing her elbow on the table and her chin in her palm.

"What?" Sae Sae closed the journal and looked at her.

"Similarities between two cases corroborate a hypothesis but they don't prove it. We need at least three points of reference."

A smile crossed Sae Sae's stern face. "You do have brains. I thought that skull was hollow inside."

"I will take that as a compliment." Aayat laughed lightly.

"We do have another case," Sae Sae cleared his throat, "Ray my fiancée, I mean my ex-fiancée, her younger sister, Amber, wandered into the jungle, too, several solar cycles back. I have her details."

"That's awful," Aayat straightened. "How old was she?"

"Eleven sun cycles old when she disappeared five cycles ago."

"Oh, poor child." Aayat's heart turned heavy. Life wasn't easy for anyone. "What do you expect to find from these cases?"

"Depends. Maybe some planetary movement, extremely high tidal waves, or anything that might be a rare phenomenon but happened every time someone crossed through the interregnum." Sae Sae scratched his chin lightly and looked at her as if asking for confirmation.

"Hmm. We can also check the time of the day when people wandered off or maybe the body type or the mental state of the person. Maybe something about the individual's inherent energy forces the portal to open."

"Probably." Sae Sae turned his face sideways and looked outside the window. Aayat followed suit. The sun was at its brightest. His shoulders relaxed as he glanced in that direction. The sight of trees put Aayat at ease, too. As if everything would turn out to be all right as long as those trees resembled the ones in her dimension.

"How are you going to find data on other people? Your aunt doesn't look like the type to share such information," she asked. Her confrontation with Errumm gave Aayat a faint idea of what that audjinn was capable of and how stubborn she could be.

Sae Sae chuckled and said, "I know those who will."

"Not good people." She eyed him suspiciously.

"How does that even matter?"

"It does. There is a line that shouldn't be crossed. I know how difficult the situation is, but I think—"

Sae Sae cut her off in between. "Don't tell me you are one of those ethical types who never cross a line and judge others for doing so." He then got up and walked to the cabinet and brought out some old printouts. "These are the details of the Djinns who disappeared over the past decade. My father collected such information for his research. But several details are still missing. We need to fill the gaps."

"Sorry about your Dad," Aayat said in a soft voice, tucking the stray strands of hair behind her ears.

"Don't be," Sae Sae said, avoiding her eyes.

"No, really. It's tough. I know. We might hate our parents at one time or the other, but they are our pillar of strength. Life feels so incomplete without them. I lived with my parents till college and Dad was mostly absent, and it irritated me so much, but he still tried to be there at least on birthdays and festivals, and we went on a family vacation once a year," she said, as she pinched her lips and studied the back of her hand.

"That sounds so, what should I say, model family type." Sae Sae gave her a brief smile, blinking away the tears swimming in his eyes.

She laughed, "Not exactly model family. Dad would always be busy on his phone, even on vacations, and mum would sulk in a corner for not getting the desired attention. By the time we came back, it was always a relief to get away from those two."

"And yet you waited impatiently for the next vacation, I bet."

"True true. Every year I promised myself to invent a course or a class to skip the vacation but, by the time the year ended, it was all I looked forward to." Aayat rubbed her hands over her arms. Thinking about her parents made her homesick. She wanted to talk to them, hear their voice, look at their face, touch them, eat a meal, and share a joke. She wanted to do everything she took for granted earlier. A hot bubble rose from her stomach and stuck in her chest.

"We will find a way soon." Sae Sae touched her right shoulder lightly.

She cleared her throat. "What else do we need to do? Anything that I can help with? As it is, I have become a burden on you two."

"Oh please, you are showing so many sides of your personality in a single day, I might get confused," Sae Sae said with a scoff, making her smile. "You are not a burden. I am glad we found you instead of the authorities."

"Me, too," she said, nodding. "So tell me, what I should do in the meantime?"

"During the time you are here, why not learn some of our ways so that if, and it's a big if, someone comes here and, you know, sees you." Sae Sae transferred some files to her chip.

"We need to fool that person into believing I am one of you." Aayat checked the file, an audiobook titled *The ways of the Djinns* and audio files of some research papers on their history.

"Yeah, something like that," he said, smiling sheepishly.

They sat in silence for a long time. Sae Sae went through the information on others who had crossed to the other world while Aayat fiddled with her chip, pronouncing the name of the book, trying to project it on the screen to check the pictures included in the book.

Adjoining Errumm's office in the district administrative headquarters was a chamber where she received important visitors. On a brown leather couch, farthest away from the bullet-proof glass door, Tenzen sat, presenting data that his friend, the undercover agent on the street 12.1, had sent. There were schedules, matched to the last *twink*, of the gang's movements, dates of their upcoming meetings, names of the people they dealt with, and the amount of the money involved in the deals. She also sent a detailed analysis of the state-of-the-art gadgets those people used, along with their pictures.

"How did you know this friend and how did she get her hands on all that?" Errumm browsed through the details.

"She infiltrated the group. I told you."

Errumm kept staring at Tenzen, making him uneasy.

He loosened the knot of his tie and said, "You mean, how do I know her? Well, do you want the truth, Madam administrator?"

"Were you planning to lie?"

Tenzen wanted to laugh, but the expression on her face forced him to stay sombre. "I worked with people at street number twelve-one. I still work with them, along with her, my friend, I mean."

"And?" She narrowed her eyes.

"I promised to trade information."

Errumm tapped her feet on the floor and said, "Go on."

"They want to know the exact date and time of the siege." Tenzen licked his lips.

"And what do you get in return?"

Tenzen scratched the back of his neck, studied the table closely, and then looked at Errumm, only to look away.

She asked again, "You get what? Money? Position? Power? All three?"

He bit his lips and stayed silent.

"Fine, you may leave. Trust goes both ways. You need to tell me everything honestly for us to work together."

"I will tell you everything, I promise, just not today." Tenzen spoke quickly lest Errumm threw him out of her office.

"Then there is nothing left to say."

He squinted. "Can't you just trust me?"

"Why should I?"

Tenzen weighed his options. He then drank some water from the cup kept on the table. "I know of your nephew's visits to street twelve-one. He has been there quite frequently in the past few days," he said as calmly as he could.

Errumm's face and ears turned red. The corner of her eyes started turning red, too. However, she stayed seated. She looked straight into Tenzen's eyes and asked, "Is that a threat?"

Tenzen regretted that he had to answer, but he had said it to gain her trust, to show her, he knew how to keep secrets. Errumm wouldn't have responded to his silence any other way.

"I mean—I meant—what I wanted to say was..." He shook his head in desperation. This wasn't the way he had imagined the conversation going. "Can you please give me a pass on this one?" he pleaded.

"That's a good way of threatening someone."

Tenzen stabbed his temple. "I wasn't doing that. I just wanted to let you know. I—"

"You what?" Errumm demanded.

"That I will never betray you." Tenzen's confidence had all but vapourised.

Errumm straightened her back and shoulders, her gaze fixed on Tenzen, who could literally feel the spark of anger shooting from her eyes.

He looked at her with a mix of fear, anxiety, and hope. He had no desire of blowing the chance away. Being on Errumm's bad side would do him no good. Moreover, he needed her help.

After a few moments of silence, Errumm said, "Fine. Begin from the beginning."

Aayat was listening to some audio files, making notes on a paper, when Feedaa hopped inside the lab wearing something that resembled a tracksuit. "Where is Sae Sae?" she asked.

"Out. What's with the outfit?" Aayat looked at her curiously.

"Sports meet. The only time school seems fun."

"Yeah?" Aayat dropped the papers in her lap.

"You not into sports and all?"

Aayat shook her head.

"What a *keefe*." Feedaa sprawled over a chair nearby. She rested her back against one of the armrests and dangled her legs over the other.

"What's that?" Aayat pointed at a bag Feedaa had dropped on the floor.

"Some clothes and other things my boring mother sent for your upkeep." Feedaa yawned.

"Tell her thanks for me."

"Sheesh. When will you stop being so formal with us?" Feedaa sat up straight. "Let's go out. Don't you get bored cramped up in this room?" She scrambled her feet noisily.

"Isn't it risky?" Aayat tightened her hair in the ponytail.

"Not at all. This lab is in the middle of nowhere. And we won't go far, just a few places here and there." Feedaa stood up, held Aayat's arms and dragged her out.

With the sun about to set, the sky had turned the shade of a burning shoal. A rainbow of flowers interspersed within various shades of green from the trees and bushes made the wilderness a sight to relish. Aayat stood breathing in the beauty of nature, taking deep breaths, filling her lungs with freshness. The cool air felt welcoming. Her skin rejoiced at the sensation.

"Let's race," Feedaa suggested. She then drew a start line in the dirt with a stick. Aayat laughed at the familiarity of the way she did it.

"Can you see that tree?" Feedaa pointed at a tree with boughs laden with pink flowers in several bunches. "It's the endpoint." She then whistled as the start cue and ran.

Aayat followed behind with all her might. They raced repeatedly. Feedaa won each time. With sweat and dirt forming a slick layer over their skin, they returned to the lab. The simple joy of being able to go out in the wilderness and enjoy a leisurely evening was enough to make Aayat happy. Her legs were covered with scratches from running through the path lined with bushes and trees, but her heart danced jubilantly.

"That was fun. I thought you were the boring type," Feedaa declared as they entered the lab. "Hope Sae Sae is not back yet. He gets angry without notice."

The two hurried to clean themselves up.

When Aayat came back, she saw Feedaa looking at the bed and clicking her tongue. "You can't sleep here. Sae Sae has got no sense. You need a proper room."

"What for?"

"Let's face it, you are going to be here for a while. Right. So you need a proper place to stay. You can't live for so many days in the middle of a hall lying on a stupid old patient bed."

Aayat shook her head slowly. "Don't worry about all that. It's fine. As it is, I am imposing on the two of you, especially Sae Sae."

"You really *are* the boring type."

Sae Sae entered the hall and joined the conversation. "Not everyone is possessed by wild spirits."

"Only the lucky ones are allowed to know the wild spirits, you *keefe*." Feedaa smacked the back of his head.

"Stop using the word all the time. You are not ten sun cycles old anymore." He hit her back and placed a box full of confections on the bed.

Chapter Twelve

The trapdoor in the kitchen of the lab led to a basement, filled with documents — both legal and illegal—machines, and gadgets. It had a huge open space in the centre with rooms on two sides. Feedaa decided one of the rooms belonged to Aayat from then on. Sae Sae lived two rooms to the right. In the middle of the night, the three of them huffed and puffed as they cleaned the floor and the walls of the room and filled it with furniture — a small wrought iron bed, a chair and a table, a mirror, and a wooden rack.

"I am so tired." Feedaa slumped on the floor of the room.

"Then go home." Sae Sae threw freshly laundered bedding on the bed.

"I don't want to. The thrill of moving into a new room is so contagious." Feedaa pulled Aayat by her hands and seated her close by on the mosaic-marble floor. She then turned towards her cousin. "Go get some food and drinks for us."

"How do you boss him? I mean, he doesn't look like he listens to people." Aayat ran her fingers through the tangled strands of her hair as Sae Sae left the room obediently.

"Everyone asks the same thing. I don't know. That's distracting," she said, pointing towards Aayat's hair. "May I touch them?"

Aayat laughed. "Sure."

"Don't they weigh your head downwards or something? Doesn't it feel weird to have something hang from the skull? How do they grow? Does everyone have them? Are they always black?"

Aayat giggled. "One question at a time, girlie."

"Girlie. Is that a cuss word?"

"No. It means young, what do you say . . . audjinn. Young audjinn. Actually, the correct word is girl, I just said it playfully."

"Aaah." Feedaa opened her mouth wide and yawned.

"Go home," Aayat suggested.

"What for? Let's sleep here."

"Like a slumber party?"

"What's that?" Feedaa enquired.

"Well, girls collect at someone's place and have fun, I guess. I wasn't invited to one ever." Aayat recalled how her classmates never invited her to any of their sleepovers. They approached her easily in times of need, but very conveniently failed to remember her when having fun.

"Let's call it that and sleep here." Feedaa climbed onto the bed, and by the time Sae Sae returned with food, she was snoring loudly.

Tenzen and Errumm sat in a small room on the roof of their office building. It had a fibre sheet overhead, and the walls were pretty thin. Both had turned off their communication devices and closed the door to prevent anyone from barging in.

Tenzen disclosed his association with the human-loving group in detail, hoping that Errumm believed him. He had no one else to turn to. Having witnessed a murder while lingering on the edges of street 12.1, he was hunted by the group and hadn't slept soundly ever since. Although he had promised them to use his position as the undersecretary of the Archives department at the administrative headquarters to bring urgent matters to their attention, he had recurrent nightmares and woke up with cold sweat every morning.

He was desperate to get on Errumm's good side. If she

believed him, he might be able to wriggle out of the situation. He had prepared for a long time to come up with a plan to eliminate the unruly Djinn group, to impress her enough to ask for a one-on- one meeting.

Now, as he ended his tale, his legs shook. He loosened the collar of his shirt and looked at Errumm, trying to figure out her thoughts, but her face gave away nothing.

"Do you plan to work as a double agent?" she asked.

"Yes and no. I will pretend to be a double agent while being loyal to you."

"And what if you betray me at the last moment?" Errumm's forehead furrowed as she looked at Tenzen with narrowed eyes.

"You still think I will?"

"Let's just discuss this further and see where we get," she replied.

"Yes, ma'am." He then showed her the pictures of every aadjinn and audjinn involved in the group. He explained where and how their department had stationed their officials to trail them and make sure that the plan was executed just as envisioned. He showed her the recordings of several meetings of the gang members and produced hard evidence of their crimes and other intent. He provided a detailed background check of all the officials involved and also showed her the additional details his friend had sent, which were a little more elaborate than the official reports.

Errumm listened without interrupting him.

Sensing her disquiet, Tenzen stopped talking and looked at her, expecting to get reprimanded for being in way over his head, but she asked him to keep going.

Once he was done, Errumm switched on her communication device to check her messages. She then poured two cups of *rokoto* and slid one towards him.

"There is one thing that I would like to tell you as a senior who has several years of experience in the field," she said. "Never trust anyone. Not even me. And the next time you discuss your plans with any person in the administration, don't divulge all details at once. Showing all your cards in one go is how you get stabbed in the back."

She then put her cup back on the table, took the files Tenzen had brought along, and left the room.

Aayat and Sae Sae made a few other changes in the bunker under the lab. The largest room was now converted into a study for research and common discussion. Sae Sae had moved his father's research on the human world there. The open space in the centre was fitted with a projector, to go through the maps and locations in detail.

Sitting on a teak-coloured rocking chair in the open area of the bunker, Sae Sae was laughing at one of Aayat's jokes when Feedaa entered.

"What's up with you two?" she asked, sounding bemused.

"Just setting up a space for work," Aayat replied.

"Wow, Sae Sae, you are sharing space with people."

"Shut up and go attend your classes," Sae Sae said with his back turned towards Feedaa.

"Who wants to be here anyway? Just give me something to wake up my senses, and I will be off." She hopped on one of the chairs beside him.

"What do you want? I'll get some," Aayat asked instead of Sae Sae, then walked towards the left corridor leading to their makeshift kitchen.

"She is making food in your house. What are you guys doing?" Feedaa mouthed the words, looking at her cousin, her eyes wide, and her hands sideways, palm upward.

"Don't use your brain too much. We are just trying to make things work." He pointed towards a counter on the wall opposite to the door with the number *36* burning brightly on the board. "Only a few days are left before the siege."

"We need to talk after I get back in the evening."

Sae Sae nodded as Aayat returned with three mugs full of some weird-looking hot liquid.

"What's this?" Feedaa asked.

"I made something like tea. I don't think it turned out well though."

"What did you use?" Sae Sae rotated the cup in his hand and tilted it a little to check the contents.

"A flower that smelled like chamomile."

"Tastes different, but okay." Feedaa sipped it greedily, chatted with the other two for a while, and left.

Aayat took the cup and sat on one of the chairs surrounding the oval wooden table, farther away from the cousins, and asked Sae Sae about their next step. She flipped through the research material, looking for a map of the city.

"First, we need to get you more acquainted with our ways of life. We will need to go out, and even if we tell people that Zenzee had lost her ability to speak after her parent's death, she would still be expected to know the basics. I hope you have gone through the material I gave you."

"Yes." Aayat nodded.

"And you need some clothes. Seeing you in aunt Errumm's clothes gives me chills. Like I can't talk to you without being courteous," Sae Sae said, crinkling his nose. Aayat had changed into a nightgown Errumm had sent and was going around in it even after the day had dawned.

"And that is not something you want to do? You want to treat me with contempt." Aayat rubbed her hands on her arm. The bunker was cooler than she expected.

"That's not what I meant. I meant you should look like you are not aunt Errumm," Sae Sae said, obviously flustered. His face and ears turned red.

"There is one more thing, if I am not imposing too much," she said, speaking slowly, pausing after every few words. "Can we please set up a proper kitchen here? I can cook a few things. Feedaa has been bending over backwards trying to feed us."

"Sure."

"I am so sorry to have put you in this spot. I really am, but like you, I'm not sure when we will find a way back to my world and I want to be of help any way I can. Also, I have always been independent, it feels awkward seeing you two work so hard while I sit and rot away in this bunker, doing nothing except mooching off you—"

"It's not your fault. It's not like you were looking to enter into our world and get trapped here." He then got up to leave and asked her to keep the communication chip close by.

"I don't know where it is," she said as she bit her lower lip. She had completely forgotten about the thing in the commotion surrounding the shifting of her room.

"Never mind. I will trace its location." He went to his room and brought another one. "This can be strapped to your wrist. It's an older model, so it has fewer functions. I reckon it would be better if you started slowly."

"I am not dim-witted. I work as a scientist in my world."

"A poor version of that, apparently. Since you can't take care of a single chip," Sae Sae quipped.

"I didn't mean to lose it. I just can't remember where I kept it. The strap makes my wrist itchy, so I prefer not to wear the thing continuously."

It was Sae Sae's turn to laugh now. "You don't understand jokes?"

"I didn't know you were joking."

"I have embedded the program that can translate your language into ours and vice versa into this chip. You can seek communication with us as well as listen to audiobooks on this device. Surfing for information would be a little problematic, as you will not understand the written data. I have uploaded some books on our customs and history for you in audio format. When I come back later, we can discuss what you learned." Having spent a lot of his time helping Feedaa with her studies, Sae Sae had become a well-practiced teacher.

"You don't think I can go back?" Aayat asked in a very low voice.

Sae Sae looked away and grunted. "I need to leave."

"You are teaching me your ways of life so that I can assimilate here without much problem." She sighed and looked at the counter. The number meant nothing if they could not find a solution by then. She would be caught or on the run. It was almost impossible to imagine spending her entire life in an alien land, to come to terms with fact that she might never be able to see her parents again. Her throat began burning.

"Don't jump to conclusions. Let's move step by step." With this, Sae Sae rushed out of the door.

As he crossed the bridge to reach the forest, Aayat's face the way it looked as he left the lab came before Sae Sae's eyes. The looming grief of losing something precious, tumbling into an unexpected situation that kept entangling more and more, was not lost to him. and then he remembered her request to set up a kitchen and sped towards the market.

An old friend approached him with a smirk on his face as he bought some kitchenware. "Wow, Sae Sae, are you and Ray already living together?"

"No," Sae Sae replied in a dry tone.

"Then what's with the shopping and all?"

"I need to cook and eat to live."

The friend had known him since college and they talked about everything he could think of—the weather, their jobs, his father, his relationship with Ray. He kept speaking but Sae Sae's mind wandered as soon as he saw someone from Street 12.1. The aadjinn who often kept silent when he visited the dingy room was walking across the road. Sae Sae paid for his things hurriedly and ran.

It was sweltering hot, and he was on his feet. Chasing after the Djinn, he had forgotten to get his car from the parking lot. It was not every day that one could see the occupants of that alley walk amongst the regular crowd. He tore through the throng of people trying not to lose sight of that Djinn, but the Djinn was quick on his feet and seemed to have melted in the crowd.

Seeing no other option, Sae Sae turned toward street number 12.1. Taking two steps at a time on the creaking staircase, Sae Sae reached the dimly lit room, panting and sweating.

"You followed me from the market. Not a very intelligent move." The aadjinn smiled through his teeth as he spoke triumphantly, "I am Jackal, by the way."

Sae Sae scratched his neck. His instincts prompted him to turn and leave, but there was much he wanted to know.

"Don't worry this is not a trap. I just saw you following me, that's all. Nothing planned." Jackal threw a bottle of cold water toward him, "Have a seat, aadjinn Sae Sae. Since you are already here, let's talk."

Sae Sae caught the bottle and inspected potential escape routes in case Jackal attacked him. There was a wide distance between his chair and the window on his left, but it was closed. Also he might not be able to reach it at a moment's notice. The other two walls had no opening. He seated himself so that the door was within his eyesight and in easy reach.

"Why don't you drink first?" Jackal leaned into his chair.

"Not thirsty." Sae Sae placed the bottle on the table.

"Really? I thought the heat was killing you." Jackal gave him a sly smile and continued. "Don't be fidgety. I just wanted to know how far you have reached on the siege business."

"It will happen sometime in the next moon cycle." Sae Sae loosened his shirt collar.

"That's it?" Jackal cocked his head and unscrewed the bottle he had given Sae Sae.

"All the departments are still not convinced. They do not have a uniform consensus." Sae Sae 's lips twitched, and a few droplets of sweat dripped down his temples. He wiped it with his finger.

"Why don't you have a sip," Jackal slid the bottle close. "Or do you want me to drink first to prove its not poisoned?"

Sae Sae turned his head and stared at the door.

"Okay then, why don't you tell me something more. Is there someone we can use to overturn the decision?" Jackal placed the cap on the bottle.

"Can't tell you everything without getting something in return." Sae Sae built as much courage in his voice as possible.

"Here," Jackal said, and brought a box containing a chip from his pocket and placed it on the table before Sae Sae. "Video from the day your father wandered into the jungle."

Sae Sae's breath stopped for a split second. Something like that existed, and he never knew. His heart banged against his chest and the room turned hotter, like he was sitting under scorching sun. Sae Sae willed himself to move and pick up the box, but his limbs won't obey, and when he did, Jackal placed his hand over it.

He had no thumb.

A shudder ran through Sae Sae.

"Which departments are they in?" Jackal looked at him.

Sae Sae's mind turned blank. He couldn't think. All he could do was see the chip under Jackal's hand.

"I said, *which departments?*" Jackal roared, bringing him back to the question.

"It's four versus three at the moment. I don't know the exact names."

"Come back with the names, and the chip is yours." Within a moment, the box was back into Jackal's pocket.

Chapter Thirteen

The blazing hot afternoon was turning into a peaceful, sleepy evening as Aayat dozed off, surrounded by torn crumpled papers she had discarded, trying to decipher some terms she had come across. Her hair was tied in a bun, and she wore one of Errumm's old tunics. Feedaa's voice reached her ears from afar. "What's all this? Why don't you go and sleep in your room?"

Aayat opened her eyes and rubbed them. "When did you come home?" She then saw the crumpled papers Feedaa was smoothing and said, "I was trying to understand time."

"How time exists? You'd solve the mystery of a lifetime. Wow." Feedaa buffed her nails on her jacket and sat.

"Not the flow of time, but how you people manage it here."

"And how exactly do we manage it here? Better or worse?"

"The duration of divisions are longer here." Aayat narrowed her eyes and scratched her head. She unclasped the bun and let her hair hang loose. She explained, knowing very well that Feedaa would not understand the concept of hours and minutes, "One day has sixteen *Rahep*. So, one *Rahep* is approximately equal to one and a half hours in my world. Also, one *Rahep* has sixty-four *twinks*, which makes one *twink* equal to one and a half minutes."

"What?"

"Nothing. Leave it. You need to understand how we divide the day for that. Anyways, how was your day?"

"Boring as usual," Feedaa said, rolling her eyes.

"Why?"

"How can I find classes interesting when there is so much going on here?" She placed her hands around Aayat's shoulders. "So, what else have you changed here?"

"Just cleaned the kitchen. We need to cook to eat. Sae Sae will bring groceries from the market on his way back. There are so few kitchen wares, and I don't yet understand how your appliances work. There are no buttons, and the surface is plain, no screens for me to touch and operate them. I thought of speaking into them, like you do into the chip, but then I didn't know the words. I tried looking for it in the audio book Sae Sae gave me, and there are five synonyms of start, but nothing worked." Aayat cleared the mess to make room for Feedaa.

"Busy day, huh." Feedaa sat on the couch beside Aayat. "And, did Sae Sae really say so?"

"Say what?"

"What else did you learn about our world?"

Aayat brought the fingertips of her right hand closer to her forehead and dipped her head a little before she said, "The customary greeting style. And also the names of the seasons. You don't divide months into weeks, I presume. There is no description of that."

"What into what?" Feedaa straightened.

"In our world, a moon cycle is called a month, which is further divided into smaller segments of seven days." Aayat raised seven fingers to show the number. "A series of seven days is called a week."

Feedaa thought for a while and said, "No, we do not complicate our lives with such divisions."

Aayat laughed at her defence. She had expected something similar.

Sae Sae calmed himself before entering the bunker. He was

still on edge. His heart had sunk into his stomach ever since he saw Jackal's thumbless hand.

"What are you two laughing at?" he asked as coldly as he could.

Feedaa replied in her usual manner, "AuDjinn talk. Nothing that concerns you."

"Why are you always here these days?" He went to the kitchen and placed the supplies on the platform.

Feedaa answered, loud enough for him to hear the words in the kitchen, "Because I don't trust you. You might choke her to death." He washed his hands and splashed some water on his face. He checked his reflection in one of the kitchen wares to ensure he looked as usual and waited for his breathing to become normal before coming into the common area.

He then asked Feedaa to repeat what she said a moment ago. She quickly retreated, saying, "Bad joke . . ."

They sat together and discussed their day for a while, sharing details of what they did, how hot the weather was and what they wanted for dinner. When Aayat went to the bathroom, Feedaa whispered, "We need to talk."

Sae Sae nodded absently. He was going out of his mind. All this tedious talk could still not make him forget the conversation with Jackal.

Making some lame excuse about the need to check the camera installation and the internet connection, they went out of the lab and walked for a while. It was dark and quiet. Not even the trees rustled. Even Feedaa was silent. As the temperature had dropped, the surroundings had become cosy. However, Sae Sae felt itchy, as if his clothes had grown thorns, pricking him all over.

They found their favourite bench underneath one of the trees lining the way to the city. Once seated, Feedaa asked, "Why are you playing house with Aayat?" Her face was almost an inch away from Sae Sae's.

"There is a video footage of the day Abee disappeared." Sae Sae scratched the paint on the seat with his left hand and placed the right one on the arm rest.

"What? Where? Who told you? Do you have it now? How is that possible?" Feedaa pulled backwards and jumped on her seat.

"Promise you won't get angry." Somehow, Feedaa's trust mattered the most.

"Sure. Just tell me more."

"I went to see someone at the street number twelve-one." Sae Sae looked at her and then away.

"Why? Why would you do that? Don't you know it's not allowed? It's dangerous. What if something happened to you? Have you lost your mind?" Feedaa took her hands out of her pockets and shook him.

"Will you please listen, for once?" Sae Sae was exasperated and exhausted. He wanted to speak his mind without having to explain his actions. "They are the only ones besides the district administration who know anything about the interregnum—I mean who have real information. I have been in touch with them for the past two years or so. A few days back, I went to them to ask about the link or something to the portal. I am sure they have one. In return, they asked me to get information on the siege Aunt Errumm's department is planning."

Feedaa lunged at him. "Don't tell me you gave it to them."

"Yes and no." Sae Sae removed her hand from his arm and looked at his feet, his toes curled inside his shoes. The stickiness in his socks became even more prominent.

"What does that even mean?" She twisted him by shoulders to make him face her.

"I know the date of the siege, but I gave them a rough approximation and not the exact date." Sae Sae looked away to avoid meeting Feedaa's eyes.

"Bravo! Should I clap for your patriotism?" Feedaa clapped

a slow, mocking clap.

Sae Sae snapped, "Do you want to hear the rest, or should I just go back to the lab?"

"Go on."

"Well, then he showed me a chip."

"Who?"

"Jackal. Have you been listening?" Sae Sae's forehead furrowed.

"Sorry, go on."

"He said it was the security footage of that day Abee disappeared. But he won't give it to me. He asked for the names of the people in the department who can be brought to their side." Sae Sae licked his lips and observed Feedaa's expression. Usually it was easy to read her mind, but at the moment she did not respond in the manner he had expected. Her face was blank. No colour change, no expression, nothing.

"He is bluffing, Sae Sae. I don't believe you fell for that." Feedaa kept her hand on his shoulder after a few moments of silence.

"I am not sure of anything anymore." A stray tear slipped from his eyes. He wiped it away hastily.

"There was a huge storm before that day. None of the cameras were working. Mum showed you all the tapes. Besides, there were some restrictions on the drones at the time. There is no probability of any footage that could have been taken using those."

Sae Sae rubbed his face with his hands.

Feedaa patted his arm lightly. "I know how you feel. Trust me, I know. But you can't lose your mind like this. If there were anything like that, mum would have handed it over to you. She did everything in her power and is still doing it—uncle was her—*is* her brother, she loved him—loves him, too. We all want him back. We all miss him," her voice became blurry. Biting her lips, she hugged Sae Sae.

They stayed like that for a while, after which Sae Sae snatched himself away from Feedaa and paced the road, stopping near a milestone.

Feedaa walked towards him. "Don't think too much. Those people are just fooling you to get more information," she said, speaking in a soothing voice. "Also, I will go through mum's files once again. I know her password. In case there is anything that had skipped our attention earlier, I will tell you. Okay?" She looked into Sae Sae's eyes and smiled.

He curved his quivering lips up in response.

Feedaa took out a huge slab of chocolate from her jacket and broke it into two. Handing Sae Sae the smaller one, she wondered out loud, "Do they have these in the other world, too? Have you read about it?"

"Can't say. Probably. They might just call it something else or maybe the preparation is different." He bit a large chunk.

"Or maybe the humans are dumb enough to have not discovered the delight of this bitter aftertaste yet."

They laughed together at Feedaa's comment.

"So what was it that you wanted to talk about?" Sae Sae asked as they retraced their steps back towards the lab. They had been out for long.

"That, oh well, nothing important." Feedaa waved her right hand in the air.

"Still, what is it?"

"Wo, umm," she said, biting her lip and looked at him from the corner of her eyes.

"What happened? How can the great AuDjinn Feedaa be at a loss of words?"

"Nothing. I just wanted to know if something is going on between you and Aayat?"

"Going on as in?" Sae Sae stopped walking and turned to face her.

"Nothing, I mean, umm, some budding romance."

"Are you crazy? Don't you use your brain at all?" Sae Sae shouted at the top of his voice.

"See, this was why I wasn't asking out loud." Feedaa quickened her steps to bring some distance between them.

Sae Sae's first impulse was to hit her, however, he simply jerked his head and replied, "It's been barely a few days since we have known her. Besides, she is a human."

"Precisely."

Sae Sae squinted. "Why are you suddenly asking such questions? You hated it when I was with Ray."

"Well, you have been behaving differently lately." Feedaa shrugged her shoulders.

"How?"

"You go out of your way to accommodate her. That's not you at all. You are not exactly the philanthropist kind."

Sae Sae scoffed. "I am not going out of my way for her. I am just trying to get rid of her as soon as possible."

"By setting up a kitchen in your lab?" She stabbed his arm with her index finger.

"We have to eat. Don't we?" He held her finger and pushed her hand aside.

"Yes, but you have had to do that for the past twenty-nine cycles, too. And you have been practically living in that lab since Aunt left." Feedaa didn't seem to be backing out easily.

"So?" Sae Sae dared her to finish the thought.

"So, my point is, you never bothered to set up a kitchen, even when Ray pleaded."

"Well, I can't exactly take Aayat to the food mart and eat with her there." Sae Sae kicked a non-existent ball.

"Who are you trying to fool?" Feedaa elbowed him and ran ahead.

"No one," Sae Sar shouted from behind and ran after her.

He understood why Feedaa was so anxious to know the details. Her parents were a living example of how things could go wrong in such relationships. He had once read a short story she wrote for a school assignment. The lead character craved a happy relationship with her father. Feedaa had only one old picture, and even that was turning grainy after seventeen sun cycles. Her father had never held her in his arms; she had never played with him in the wilderness like Sae Sae and his father. None of the family members talked of him. Errumm never told her what he was like. All she knew was that it was a mismatched relationship, and by the time Errumm realised it, she was already carrying Feedaa. Her parents were not in the favour of birthing the child but adamant as she was, Errumm stood firm on her decision.

Sae Sae remembered how she had scribbled "What is a father" on her notebook and then scratched it quickly, sensing his presence.

"You two are back? Good. There are a few things that I noticed while comparing the cases of disappearances," Aayat started without so much as hello as soon as the two entered the bunker. "There has always been a storm a day before anyone entered the interregnum." She crossed the room to come close to them and spoke.

"We know that," Feedaa retorted, still standing.

"And it usually coincides with the blue blood moon." Aayat joined her fingers and the thumb of both her hands to make a circle, representing the moon.

"What's a blue blood moon?" Sae Sae asked sliding chairs out for Feedaa and himself.

"You need to understand the concept of months for that. Okay, let's begin with what you might understand. Do you know what a lunar eclipse is?" Aayat took her usual seat on the study table. A wide dark-brown lounge chair fitted with soft cushion and covered with aqua coloured floral fabric had become her favourite.

"Never heard of it." Sae Sae shook his head.

"Well, you must have studied about the sun and the moon. Right?" Aayat dragged the chair closer to the table around which Feedaa and Sae Sae sat.

Both cousins nodded, still looking at Aayat.

"So there are times when the shadow of the earth falls on the moon, making it completely invisible to our eyes."

"The curtain drawing. Yes, we know that it happens with the Sun, too." Sae Sae crossed his arms on his chest and leaned on the chair.

"Exactly. A blood moon is when the light of the sun falls on the moon, making it look red to the observer's eye. And this always happens on a full moon night," Aayat continued, using the diagram she had already drawn on the digital writing pad Sae Sae gave her, to explain the phenomenon, in case, they did not know what eclipse was.

"What's so strange about curtain on the moon? Doesn't it happen like every now and then?" Feedaa looked at her cousin.

"Yes, but it is not always total. Most times, the shadow of the earth is partial. However, what she is talking about occurs only when the moon is completely hidden by the shadow of the earth and the light of the sun, reflected by the moon looks the colour of blood." Sae Sae explained the phenomenon in detail.

"So we have it here, too?" Feedaa clapped her hand.

"Yes, and if you'd attend your classes instead of wasting time here and there, you would know that," Sae Sae snarled. "Now what's blue whatever moon that you were talking about?" he turned to Aayat.

"For that, we need to understand the division of year in my world."

"Go on," he nudged.

"We know that one sun cycle is completed in three hundred and sixty-five days. I hope you calculate it similar." Aayat looked at them expectantly.

"Three hundred and sixty-five days and three and a half *Rahep*." Sae Sae gave the exact duration.

"Yes. The additional hours give us one more day every fourth year. But that is not the point here."

Sae Sae adjusted in his chair, coming a little closer.

"So, in our world, a year, or a sun cycle as you call it, is divided into twelve parts called months. We do not go by the moon cycle over there. I mean every culture does have a count, but the official calendar is fixed regarding the number of days and months. Am I clear?"

"Yes, you have twelve equally divided parts in a solar cycle," Sae Sae repeated.

"Not quite equally divided." Aayat wrote the names of months and the number of days in each on the digital pad and projected it on the screen for clarity.

"We can't read your language," Feedaa said as she saw the chart.

"I know, just look at it like it's a drawing. We interpret artwork all the time." She then thought for a moment and wrote numbers beside the names of the month and gave the pen and pad to Sae Sae and said, "Write down the numbers in your language." She then pointed towards January and asked him to write the numbers 1 and 31 on the side. "This is the first month in our calendar, and it has thirty-one days."

"How did you decide that it was the first month?" Feedaa asked.

"How is that important right now? Stop wasting time," Sae Sae snapped.

Aayat continued explaining the calendar. "Now, as you see, our calendar is independent of the solar and lunar cycles. So there are times when we have two full moons in the same month. The months with thirty-one days are the most likely to witness the phenomenon. When that happens, the second full moon of the month is called the blue moon. And if by chance there is a total lunar eclipse on the second full moon which makes the moon turn red to the eyes of the observer, then it is known as the blue blood moon."

Aayat looked at them waiting for a response, but no one stirred.

"So, you mean to say, every time someone crossed the interregnum, it was a blue blood moon," Sae Sae spoke after a few minutes of silence.

"Not every time, but it's one of the common factors in several occurances."

"But isn't it, I mean it seems like a rare occurrence." He looked at her.

"Yes, and so is entering an alternate dimension," Aayat continued. "There might be other triggers too, but this is what I have concluded up till now."

"You are a smart creature." Sae Sae looked at her and smiled.

Chapter Fourteen

When Aayat got up to fetch water in the wee hours of the morning, she saw Sae Sae reading the constellation charts projected on the wall. A few tattered old books with yellowed pages were open in front of him on the table. The files of those who'd disappeared in the jungle and were suspected to have passed the interregnum were displayed beside the constellation chart on the wall. His eyes were drooping, and he almost slouched on the seat, ready to slip any moment.

"Why don't you go and rest, and we will go over the data together in the morning," she went near him and said.

"I can't sleep." He rubbed his nose and looked at her through drooping eyelids.

"You look pretty much wasted to me." She closed the books on the table.

"That's just the night taking its toll." Sae Sae sat up straight. "*Accha.*"

"What?" He drank some water from a bottle placed on the table.

"Nothing." She smiled.

"What was your life like, Aayat? Before you ended up in this mess?" he asked, as if coming back to his senses after a long time.

"What was my life like?" The question seemed so alien at the moment. "Well, just the regular boring one like everyone else. Work, eat, sleep, repeat." Aayat sat in front of him. It was strange. They were spending a lot of time together, talking, discussing. The animosity had decreased, although Aayat still felt that Sae Sae was far from considering her a friend.

"That's it?"

"Yeah, pretty much." Aayat smacked her lips playfully and was surprised at her own behaviour.

"That can't be true." He turned off the projector and blinked his eyes repeatedly, probably to moisten them after staring at the screen for so long.

"Why?"

"You are smart," he said in a matter-of-fact tone. Aayat smiled inwardly. Sae Sae wasn't one to complement easily.

"Is that a compliment?" she confirmed; her heart fluttered like a butterfly.

"Of course, it is. You figured out the blood whatever moon thing in just a matter of a few *raheps*. I'd consider that smartness." He cocked his head.

"It's just a coincidence. I recalled a news article I read in my world on the morning of the day I landed here. It said something about the blue moon occurrences, so I checked it out. But it isn't the only trigger." Aayat tucked a tendril of hair behind her ear. She knew Sae Sae hated the sight of her stray hair.

"What do you mean by not the only trigger?"

Aayat looked at him, saying, "We have access to a total of five cases, mine, your dad's, Amber's, and two others. Three of them occurred on a blood blue moon night. Considering it's a rare phenomenon, we can factor it as one of the triggers. But the other two cases, including Amber's, occurred on usual nights. I checked the planetary alignments and the constellations. Amber disappeared when the moon was waxing and the other one disappeared when it waned."

Sae Sae stayed silent. Aayat scanned his face, trying to figure out what was going on in his mind. His eyes twitched and he thinned his lips. He looked at her and then away. He fiddled with the book in his lap, then exhaled audibly. "I hope we find some answers soon. I am sure you want to go back to your boring life. You have a family, a career, new heights you want to soar up to and probably a lover."

Aayat wanted to tell him that she wasn't as scared or lonely as she'd first felt. And that she had come to like his and Feedaa's company and would remember them forever, wherever she might be. She also wanted to clarify that she was single, but then decided to stay quiet. The way he sighed at the word *lover* made her blood rush with double the speed. The contortion on his face made her happy.

Sae Sae paced around the room a little, checked some files, and left, while she stayed there, working, trying to figure out something, anything, that would work in their favour.

For the next few days, Aayat stayed hunched up on the table with papers, weather reports, tidal charts, planetary alignment charts, and everything else that she could think of. The reports were mostly incomprehensible to her because of the language difference, so Sae Sae translated them for her when they sat together while she scribbled the notes on pieces of paper. The complications of dealing with their gadgets where most functions and programs were in a different language prompted her to go old school and use paper and pen for most of her work, instead of the artificially intelligent technology.

The task gave her a sense of purpose as well as an assurance that she was doing everything in her power to return to her world and soon they might find a way. It was the only thing that let her sleep at night. She might have gotten used to staying with the cousins, but this wasn't her home. Living there felt didn't sit well.

"Let's take her out somewhere," Feedaa suggested one evening. "She must be going out of her mind trapped in this bunker."

"Where?" Sae Sae asked.

"Am I seeing and hearing things correctly? You agreed without much ado?" Feedaa patted her ears to check if they were working properly.

"Shut up. I am not a tyrant. We all can see the dark circles underneath her eyes and the sallow complexion on her face."

Aayat looked at him, her eyes wide. She had no idea that he noticed her so much. Her heart fluttered. She chided it. This was no time and place to blush. Feedaa had a keen sense of observation.

"Let's go to Xanso then," Feedaa suggested.

"Xanso?"

"It's a family property that we own jointly. Our grandparents named us the trustees," Feedaa explained.

"You have become trustees at such young ages?"

Feedaa narrated the tale as they got into the car. "Well, our grandmother, the one who chafed for action, acquired some land from the award money she received and planted several hundreds of trees in it. You know, to make the land clean and green, but she was not sure that the crusade would go on once she was gone, so she devised this method. She named us joint trustees of the property on the condition that it would never be used for residential or industrial purposes. Just for planting trees and maybe use the products for the benefit of the occupants of Faejenda or by the world in association. The moment either of us deviates, we would no longer remain the trustees,"

"Don't you get tired of speaking so much?" Sae Sae intervened. "It's such a boring story."

Aayat smiled and said, "Not at all."

The property was on the opposite end of the city. Sae Sae drove the car at lightning speed to make sure no one noticed Aayat. At places they had to stop or slow down, he asked her to duck.

They reached a huge gate that opened after scanning the

number plate of his car.

"Aren't there any caretakers or guards here?" Aayat enquired.

"No need. Our security system is the best, and those who take care of the trees, and everything leave after their work hours are over. It is mostly empty at night." Feedaa rolled down the window. "You know why I suggested coming here today?"

"Why?" Aayat asked, despite knowing very well that Feedaa would answer even without any prodding,

"You'll know when we reach it." Feedaa laughed at her own joke.

Sae Sae parked his car in the open, and the three hopped out. It seemed like a huge maze of green all around. The other two slithered across it with ease as Aayat followed closely. She removed her scarf and let the breeze blow through her hair and over her face. She had never bothered to stop and admire the air. However, being trapped in a bunker for so many days made her realise its importance. Her body cooled instantly under the touch of air, the muscles seemed to relax, and her mind loosened up, too. She was overjoyed just to be able to stand in the open and breathe.

How many things we take for granted in our life. Everything we receive free of cost is worth celebrating.

"Hey, where are you, lost?" Feedaa shook her shoulders. "Come on, we haven't reached the best part of the place yet." She then took Aayat's hand and picked up speed, dragging her along.

The sky above was clear and starry. And the expanse of land before them was huge. The enormity of the place made Aayat feel insignificant.

Sae Sae stood in front of what seemed like a misshapen pond surrounded by stones and rocks of all shapes and sizes. His ocean blue eyes searched something in oblivion. The reflection of the full moon above floated freely in the water below.

Aayat went and stood beside him, "what are you thinking?"

"Nothing, no one is thinking anything tonight. We are here to have fun, and I will kill anyone who ruins that for me." Feedaa came from behind and pushed Aayat into the pond. She fell with a splash. A moment later, Feedaa and Sae Sae joined her. The three played like little children for a long time—bobbing up and down, giggling, laughing, and splaying water all around. They took turns diving in and checking who could stay underwater the longest.

Sae Sae was the first to get out of the pond. He disappeared for a while and came back with towels and robes. Feedaa led her to the changing room at the end of the fence. A few dresses hung in the wardrobe. Aayat chose one and changed.

The two strolled to the farthest end of the property, where a high-definition astronomical telescope stood proudly. Sae Sae was already there, fine tuning the lenses. They took turns watching the planets and the constellations and marvelled over the genius of the maker of the universe.

"This is the first time I have had so much free time at hand," Aayat said suddenly.

"You were too busy in your world?" Feedaa passed her a purple sweet and sour candy she had miraculously produced from her pocket.

"Yes, it's a competitive place to be. And when you are the only one who could fulfil all the expectations of your parents, the pressure multiplies exponentially."

"Your parents forced you to choose a career?" Feedaa asked, unable to mask the surprise in her voice.

"Not exactly. But they are both accomplished in their fields. They wouldn't have wished for me to wander off track."

"And become like Feedaa." Sae Sae completed the sentence

and laughed.

"Not at all, she is a nice person."

"Don't pamper her. She is already out of her mind."

"I am not," Feedaa retorted.

"Yes, you are." Sae Sae ran away from Feedaa and wiggled from afar.

"Why do you guys fight like cats and dogs all the time?" Aayat couldn't help asking.

"Then what do you expect me to do with this good for nothing aadjinn? Who can talk to him politely? Have you tried doing so? Do you think he deserves to be treated with respect?" Feedaa stuck out a tongue at him.

"He is not that bad now. Stop saying things like that."

"You think he is a good person. Wow. That's a first. I have never heard anyone defending Sae Sae." Feedaa then touched Aayat's forehead. "You are not sick or something, are you?"

Aayat laughed in reply and moved along the periphery of the high walls lining the property. "So, what are you guys going to do with this place?"

Feedaa detailed her plans for the property. "Plant trees, take care of the environment, and make sure they are always here to purify the air."

"And you? What are your plans for the place?" Aayat turned to Sae Sae, who had crawled back slowly.

"Not thought about anything yet. Feedaa can do whatever she likes. I have no interest in plants and all."

"They are important for our survival Sae Sae," Feedaa scolded him like a schoolteacher.

"Of course they are, Feedaa," he replied with a sarcastic smile.

Aayat's hair had dried and settled on her face, sticking wherever it found room. She saw Sae Sae eyeing her closely, and her hands automatically went to the tangled black mess. She cleared her face and turned away.

Chapter Fifteen

The morning was stormy. Thick grey clouds covered the sky, making it almost as dark as the night. The temperature dropped by several degrees in a matter of a few hours.

Errumm received an urgent request for communication from Sae Sae on her way to the office.

"I need to see you," he said in a hurry, his words ramming into one another and making the pronunciation unclear.

"Swing by the office."

"I don't trust those people. Someone might overhear."

Errumm knew Sae Sae had several reasons to not trust the people in the administration. "Then?" she asked him for the place of his choice.

"Somewhere far away from the maddening chaos, at a place that no one else knows."

Errumm grunted her approval and disconnected the call.

Amidst pouring rain and a lashing thunderstorm, she reached the rendezvous point. Errumm got out from her car and walked towards a small cave, her heels digging deep in dirt as the hem of her pants caked with soil. The small stones and pebbles scattered in the way threatened to take her down with a fall before she reached her destination. "What is it that you wanted to talk about in this wilderness?" she spoke through her teeth as soon as she saw him.

"Are you still planning the siege?" Sae Sae stood at the mouth of the cave, holding a huge, black umbrella in his hand.

"Yes." Errumm pushed past him and entered the cave. She had been there often enough to know the cave held a few folding chairs.

"Which departments do not support you?" Sae Sae followed her in, closed the umbrella and rested it on the moss-ridden, dark green wall, near the cave's mouth.

"What is it to you?" She stretched out on one of the chairs and sat. It creaked as she adjusted her position. The paint on the wrought iron legs of the chairs was coming off and it was corroded at the exposed places.

Splashes of rain droplets entered through the open mouth of the cave, drenching the upper layer of Errumm's clothing. She lifted the chair and moved further inside.

"I need to pass on the information to the other side." Sae Sae squinted his eyes and stood close to her.

She looked at him with a mix of anger and bewilderment. "Are you in your right mind, Sae Sae?"

"Yes."

The noise of rain droplets falling on the tree leaves outside overtook the silence in the cavity of the cave as none of them spoke for a while. Finally, Errumm got up. "I thought I was coming to see my nephew. You are not him."

"Aunt, please . . ." He looked at her with the eyes of a little puppy, reminding her of his childhood.

Warmth spread through her chest. The desperation in his husky, torn voice stopped Errumm. Her heart ached at his tone. She had held him in her hands the day he was born. She loved him, took care of him, watched him grow up. "What's going on, kiddo?" she asked.

He hadn't heard anyone call him that in a long time. Sae Sae cleared his throat several time before speaking and blinked his eyes repeatedly, "I need the information."

"To trade it with people who operate from the street number twelve-one. I understand that much. What I don't understand, my child, is your association with them." Errumm touched his cheek with affection.

Sae Sae didn't know where to start. So much had happened in the past few years. He had looked up to Errumm to answer all his questions, but at times she was too busy to call upon him. She also had her hands tied with the confidentiality clause, so she couldn't share all the required information with him, and when she answered, he wasn't satisfied with what she said. He needed something concrete, something to help him take the next step, move forward, and bring his father back. That something, Errumm could not provide. She wasn't supposed to encourage him to engage in illegal activities. Tired of the waiting and uncertainty, he'd turned to those who answered him.

"Do you trust me?" he asked. His chest rose and fall with every breath as he looked at his aunt.

"Of course I do. You are the smartest person I know." She smiled, her eyes mirroring his emotions.

"Then, trust me one more time," he pleaded.

"Just tell me why you want the names. I need to be sure you are safe. That's my priority." Errumm spoke softly.

"It's a long story."

"I have time." She stretched out to reach for another chair and patted the seat.

"The human female that you met that day found an interesting correlation between the time people crossed the interregnum and planetary alignment. One day before the crossing, almost every time, there had been a storm. It happened in both the dimensions." He looked at Errumm, who nodded in conformation of her understanding. "The second correlation she found was—three out of five crossings occurred on blue blood moon night," Sae Sae explained.

"What's that?"

"Complete shadow of Earth on the moon on the second full

moon of the month."

"Second full moon of what?" Errumm narrowed her eyes.

"It's a concept of their world. They have their solar cycles divided into a fixed number of days. Each part is called a month and at times, a longer part sees two full moons. Are you following?"

"Not exactly, but go on."

"So, three incidents occurred on such days, but two others didn't. I need to find about others who have crossed the worlds to complete the theory." He looked at Errumm, fishing for words to convey his exact thoughts.

"What theory?"

"The triggers that open the portal. If we know for sure what opens the portal, we can prepare in advance or at least know what to expect when . . . I don't know. It's something we have been working towards. Nothing concrete, but at least a start, a hope." Sae Sae expected her to reprimand him, but she just sat there staring at the end of the cave. Stalactites hung from its roof as water dripped through them onto the stalagmites rising from the floor.

"You think that will make a difference?" Errumm asked, still staring at the slimy structures in front of her.

"Can't say, but it is better than not trying at all."

"Do you trust this human?" Errumm questioned him.

"She wants to go back. This is not her home. I want her to go back, too. She doesn't belong with us. Also, she has brains. It took her a matter of few *raheps* to discover the phenomenon that occurred the night she was transported here. She has a mind for discovering things, and she understands how things work. If nothing else, at least she can form theories and reason them out." Sae Sae licked his lips.

"What did she work as in her world?"

"Some sort of scientist."

Errumm laughed at his answer. "One of your kind?"

"Yeah, well, their techniques are pretty outdated if you ask me," Sae Sae laughed with her.

"Then why did you believe in her theory?"

He exhaled sharply. "Because it was something I never caught on to before today, and it involved an occurrence that I could never understand because of the way our calendar works."

"Never thought I'd see this day."

"What day?" He stared at her.

"When you will accept that someone did what you could not or might not have been able to do." Errumm smirked.

"It's not my fault our calendar is faulty."

"Sure it is."

Sae Sae clicked his tongue, and Errumm smiled at the resemblance between Feedaa and him.

"Will you tell me the names of the departments now?"

Errumm listed the names. "The department of Internal investigation, department of visual security control, and the department of supplies, all three are opposed to the idea of the siege."

"What has the department of supplies got to do with this?"

"I have a hunch, but it needs to be confirmed first, nothing that concerns you though." She took out a packed vegetable wrap from her bag and handed it to Sae Sae. He looked haggard, like he wasn't eating or sleeping well.

"Thank you so much. I owe you one. I really really do." Sae Sae held Errumm's hands tightly and gave a wide-toothed smile.

"You don't owe me anything. Just make sure you are safe, and this conversation stays between us." Errumm looked outside. The rain hadn't stopped but had slowed down. She checked the time and then walked out, instructing Sae Sae to leave some time after her.

Aayat woke up later that morning to find Sae Sae gone and the clouds roaring in rebellion. Glad to be alone, she tiptoed to the study and shifted through a few pages but was soon distracted by the thoughts clouding her mind.

When in doubt, run, it clears your mind. She remembered her dad's words.

Would it be safe to go out on my own? 'Will I create any trouble?

She went to her room, changed into Errumm's clothes, tied her hair tight with the only hair tie she had, and then looked for a cap or something similar. If she was able to hide her hair, she could take the chance to go out for a run. Rain seemed safer as fewer people would be on the track. She was debating whether to enter Sae Sae's room to look for what she needed when he returned.

"What are you doing here?" he asked.

"I—I—cap—run—I . . . ."

"Something happened in your sleep? What are you stuttering?" Sae Sae opened the door of his room and asked, "Do you need anything?"

Aayat swallowed her inhibition. "I wanted to go out for a run."

"In this rain?" He pointed to the window. Rain pelted like there was no tomorrow. Even the air inside the bunker had turned damp and heavy.

"There will be fewer people," she reasoned.

"You don't fear getting caught?"

"I do, but I just, just wanted to get some fresh air."

Sae Sae gestured for her to come inside the room. It was pretty empty. A single wooden bed with a swan carved on the right side of the headrest stood near the right wall, neatly made. A small cupboard, a study table, and a wooden chair were aligned to the opposite wall. The room was spotlessly clean and devoid of any pictures or mementos. The walls were dull hay coloured. Sae Sae took out a jacket from his cupboard, which felt like plastic on touch. "Wear this over your clothes. Will prevent you from soaking." He also handed her something like swimming goggles to save her eyes from the rain. Pointing at the top of her head, scrutinising her hair, he said, "That thing is really distracting. What are you going to do about it?"

"Huh?"

"You can't go out like this." He came out of the room, Aayat scuttling close behind, and then went around the entire bunker, going into rooms, coming back out , looking at her with exasperated eyes. He said, "You are such a pain. Just go and run on the terrace. It's huge enough for you to run laps. I will disable the surrounding security cameras for a while."

"You can do that?"

"White noise. I will produce some white noise to block the frequency at which they record."

Aayat reached the terrace, taking two steps at a time.

The lab was huge and in the middle of nowhere. She hadn't even seen all the rooms yet. Though she wanted to explore the place, the fear of making Sae Sae angry prevented her from wandering off. Covering the entire lab, the terrace seemed more expansive than she had imagined.

The rain fell hard, huge droplets that felt like pebbles being dropped from the sky. The wind howled, making Aayat's clothes flutter. Her face and the back of her hands were soaked within a few minutes. She could almost feel her teeth chattering, but she loved the experience nonetheless. She had been confined to the lab for long. She wiped her face and looked around. Huge trees lined the perimeter of the lab on all sides. Beyond them were the mountains. Himalayas, she thought and then smiled. The clouds roared ferociously and drops of rain pelted even faster, hitting her like whiplashes now. Were she in her right mind, she would have rushed downstairs, but nothing was right anymore. Aayat checked if her jacket was fastened properly, adjusted the goggles over her eyes, and began running.

Chapter Sixteen

Even if his loyalties lay at other places, Sae Sae reckoned keeping in touch with Jackal could prove fruitful. After mulling over the pros and cons of his association with the human-loving side for some time, he visited the dingy room on street 12.1 to have a long-awaited discussion with Jackal.

Sae Sae seated himself in front of the dubious inhabitant of the room, his back stiff and hands balled into fists as he named the two departments against the siege. "The department of supplies and the department of social services."

"Are you sure those are the only department?" Jackal scratched his chin, sitting across the table from him in a pale yellow shirt with brownish blotch on the collar and nearby areas.

"There may be more, but these are the ones I know about."

"How do I know that you are not lying?" Jackal scrutinized him with narrowed eyes.

"Exactly." Sae Sae smiled slyly, leaned on the chair, and crossed his arms across his chest. "There are risks that we all must take. Don't you think?" He noticed the old scars around Jackal's nose and around his jaw line. Jackal's neck bore some fresh scratches too.

"You truly are Errumm's nephew, aren't you?"

"You had a doubt?"

Jackal got up and walked towards the window. He had a slight limp. A fresh one, Sae Sae thought. He had disappeared from the market in the blink of an eye. He couldn't have done so with a limp.

"What happened to your leg?"

"The same thing that can happen to you if you mess with the wrong people," Jackal replied with his back towards Sae Sae. He lifted the patched drape from the window and peered outside. His head bobbed from side to side.

"There are people even you fear. That's interesting." Sae Sae tried to mask his fear with sarcasm.

"What is it that you want?" Jackal came back to the table. "The video clip?"

"No."

Jackal cocked his head. "Then what?"

"Name and date of disappearance of Djinns from your side."

Jackal shifted in his chair and studied his chipped fingernails. "Why?"

Sae Sae turned red, more in fear than in anger. *What if Jackal refuses to cooperate?* He said out loud, "What is it to you? You got what you wanted." His legs trembled. He stiffened to stop them from showing his emotions so transparently.

"Who are you doing this for? The human female hiding in your bunker?" Jackal straightened and faced Sae Sae, his face looking as calm as the sea before launching a mighty typhoon.

Sae Sae's heart stopped beating for a moment. His head felt dizzy as the room darkened. Everything stood still.

Breathe Sae Sae, breathe.

Jackal came closer and whispered, "You thought no one knew?"

Sae Sae kept silent. He tried swallowing the saliva in his mouth but somehow couldn't. *How — how — how? How can this person know about Aayat? Something is definitely off. Was he following me? Is anyone else following me? Has he stationed his people near the bunker? Are they still there? Is Aayat safe? I need to get out of here.*

Sae Sae felt his leg shaking under the table. His toes curled. He blinked repeatedly to bring himself back to focus and locked his jaws tight to prevent his teeth from chattering.

Several thoughts buzzed in his mind.

Should I run? Should I kill him? Can I kill him? Will I be able to survive after killing him? Who else knows?

Jackal said something. Sae Sae saw his lips moving but the voice did not reach him.

"Don't worry, I am not going to tell anyone. You scratch my back, I scratch yours," Jackal said, grinning. This time Sae Sae could hear him. He then drummed his fingers on the table and looked at Sae Sae curiously. "You really underestimated our lot."

"Just give me what I want. I can't sit here and listen to you the whole day." Sae Sae swallowed hard and regained his composure or at least pretended to.

"Of course, my dear aadjinn, we all have a life to live. Two names in exchange for two departments. Fair enough?"

Sae Sae scanned the files he received digitally and left the room, his heart still beating in his throat.

Aayat was humming a tune while browsing through some videos on the chip Sae Sae had given her, sitting in the common area of the bunker. She was wearing one of his shirts which hung loosely on her thin frame. Suddenly she burst into laughter. Sae Sae saw her wiping off tears from the corner of her eyes—happy tears.

He transferred the file to her device and went to his room without saying anything.

"What's this?" She knocked at the door of his room and entered.

"Information on two more aadjinns who disappeared." He sat at his study table, hands on the top, his fingers interlaced tightly.

"Where did you get that from?" she asked, taking a seat in front of him.

"Does it matter?" The where and who, both had Sae Sae going out of his mind with fear. He didn't need any more reminders.

"No. Did you check the planetary alignment on the days these people disappeared? Did it coincide with anything we know? I mean do they corroborate our theory, or do they refute it?" Aayat projected the files on the opposite wall.

"Yes."

"And?"

"No such thing." Sae Sae was on edge. His replies were brusque.

"Is everything all right?" Aayat looked at him. Her gaze moved all over his face.

"Yes."

"Doesn't seem like."

"Focus on the work." He dashed out of the room. The breathing space seemed to be shrinking.

What am I going to do? Should we move from here? But go where? Aunt Errumm's place? But that would put her and Feedaa in danger too? What should I do? What should I do?

Warning Aayat didn't seem right, but he needed to confide in someone, he needed someone to console him, to tell him that it would be all right, and more than that he needed someone he could trust. He paced the common area with long impatient strides. He scratched his hand and neck and then his legs. Something seemed to be piercing his skin. Hiccupping, he looked around restlessly when Aayat entered shouting, "Sae Sae, Sae Sae, there is something else we could do?"

"What?"

"Are you all right?"

"How many times are you going to ask the same question?" he snapped.

"As many times as you lie."

Sae Sae gave a fake laugh. The cooling seemed to have stopped working. He felt hot and sweaty as the human female standing in front of him stared directly at his face as though she could peep right into his heart and understand the disturbance caused within.

She then turned and went inside without saying a word. He slumped on a couch near the corridor leading towards the kitchen and kept sitting for a long time, trying to tell himself that there is a way out of this mess, and he would definitely find one.

It was only after Feedaa came that he realised how much daylight he had wasted.

"Why do you look like a slaughter animal that knows we are going to eat it in a few hours?" She threw a crumpled chocolate wrapper at him.

He peered around to check whether Aayat was out of earshot and then whispered, "Someone knows about her, I mean *they* know about her, that she stays with us, and that she is not an audjinn."

Feedaa's eyes turned to twice their size. "How do you know? Are you sure they meant Aayat and not someone else? Who told you? What are we going to do now? Oh God, Sae Sae, what are we going to do?"

His mind turned blank, everything seemed to have vanished, all ideas, all thoughts and a sharp pain accompanied by loud drumming sound took the place. Getting the news off his chest reduced some of the congestion, but the tension in his mind was still intact.

What are we going to do?

Tenzen visited Errumm's house, wearing a pale mint green suit. He looked confident and gave her a brilliant smile. For the first time, she noticed how charming he was when not anxious or worried. Errumm took him to the greenhouse on the roof. Tiny colourful flowers and kitchen herbs grew in tubs and flowerpots.

"This is where I usually come when I need peace," she told him while admiring the lilies.

"It's a beautiful place to be."

"Yes, and wait till it's winter and the sunlight filters through the glasses. You would love to spend mornings here." Errumm signalled him to sit.

A round wrought iron table, polished white, was welded to the floor of the greenhouse. Four chairs surrounded it. Flower motifs were exquisitely carved on the tabletop. "My father loved making such designs. He was a metal craftsman. The basement of this place still houses all his tools and incomplete pieces," she added with nostalgia.

"He had a great eye for art, I see."

Errumm smiled in response and sat on the chair in front of him. "So, where are we with all the preparations?"

"Am I supposed to trust you?" Tenzen questioned with a look that contradicted his words.

Errumm laughed in response. "That depends on you. Doesn't it?"

"Well, then I choose to trust you completely in this project." He smiled and settled in his chair. "As we discussed earlier, the siege will be executed in four different stages, the groundwork for which has already started. We have placed all our informants in position, just to make sure that the movements that we traced are still rhythmic and there is no chance of missing out on the operation because someone didn't move as we had expected."

He took a sip of water and continued. "We won't be using the drone cameras or magnetic identifiers, as they can be traced."

"So, what are you going to do now?"

"We will go old school." Tenzen's eyes gleamed. "We will use pocket cameras. Our people will wear them on their shirts."

"Do we still have them?"

"A few old ones. We can always make them again to suit our needs. No one expects people to use such old technology when newer, easier, and better ones are in place." Tenzen looked expectantly at Errumm, who thought of praising him but then the strict authoritarian in her raised her head, preventing her from complementing Tenzen till the work was actually taken care of.

"Okay." Her expressionless, brusque reply seemed to disappoint him. "Then what?" she asked, looking out the glass pane.

"This is something we need to discuss." Tenzen looked at her and then all around them. He then came closer and whispered something into her ear that brought Errumm's world crashing down.

CHAPTER SEVENTEEN

Rain continued for a week—no sun, no calm and quiet. Lashing thunderstorms made the thick heavy droplets pour from the grey clouds, accompanied by fierce, blinding lightning. They hit the window glass noisily. Feedaa hadn't visited the bunker since the rain started. Aayat and Sae Sae ate and slept on the couch and the rocking chair in the common area. Aayat's hair had turned into a tangled mess, and her face had lines from sleeping on papers.

"Is there a possibility that we have the data wrong?" Aayat checked one of the files on the digital pad.

"How?"

She projected the data on the wall. Seven columns, each filled with information about the Djinns who had disappeared in the past few years, came alive. She had developed some symbols for commonly used words—*eclipse*, *thunderstorm*, and *energy*, as well as the names of the Djinns who disappeared to aid her presentation.

Sae Sae turned towards the wall. His gaze moved upwards and downwards and from left to right several times, before asking, "What is it that I am missing?"

"See, there was a storm in five cases. And blood blue moon in three. Which means these triggers are not universal."

"We have already gone through that."

"I know, but the problem is, others do not have a common factor. There is nothing that unites the cases that do not fall in these categories." She scratched her hair.

"Maybe you need a bath and a good sleep. Then look at the

thing with a fresh eye," he suggested.

"There is one more thing. I have studied the map of the jungle in detail. There are a total of seven spots your father marked, and you found me at one of these. Right?"

"Yes."

Aayat cleared the table and displayed a digital version of the map on it. She then marked the points. "Now look at this." She projected a hologram of the Big Bear constellation in the air, approximately a foot above the map, and then moved it to align the position of the stars.

"What is this supposed to mean?"

"The spots for possible portal opening form the shape of a constellation."

Sae Sae studied the map and the hologram and the alignment of the marked spots in the form of the constellation. He walked all around the map in silence, playing with a button on his sleeves.

"You are seeing things that are of no use. Even if it forms a bunch or a design, what use is it to us? Just go and rest." He held her arms and stood her up.

Aayat had no proof that her thoughts made sense. It was still a hunch and arguing with Sae Sae meant she needed more information, logic and at least one theory to back her up. She would also need an example to demonstrate that she was correct. Since it was not possible at the time, she left the room without much ado.

"Wake up, sleepyhead." Feedaa came and woke Aayat just after dusk. "What have you been up to?"

Aayat looked at her and squinted as if seeing her for the first time. She was back in her world in the dream, and waking in the bunker felt disorienting. All the familiar things were suddenly gone. She rubbed her eyes and the corner of her mouth.

"What time is it?"

"Eleventh *Rahep*." Feedaa checked her chip. "Where is the mad cousin of mine?"

"Who? Oh, him. Don't know." Aayat looked around the room. "Did the rain stop?"

"Yes, that's why I'm here."

"What did you do today? It's been almost seven days since I saw you." Feedaa helped Aayat out of bed and went into the kitchen with her.

"Working on a way to get out." Aayat gulped a glass of water in one go.

"Found anything yet?"

"Everything seems so confusing, as if mixed up in a jumble. I need to clear my head. Shall we go somewhere? Fresh air might do me some good."

Someone knows we are hiding a human in the bunker. Sae Sae's words sent a chill down Feedaa's spine when she heard them for the first time. What if they harmed her, she had asked frightfully.

"Umm, why don't we jog around the bunker? Is it big enough to give you the exercise needed?"

"What?" Aayat looked at her and squinted again.

Feedaa scratched her temple. *What's wrong with her? Something doesn't feel right. Does she know that Jackal knows? Did Sae Sae tell her?*

"First, tell me what all you have come to know." Feedaa sat on the kitchen counter, while Aayat was working at chopping the vegetables and mixing the dough for the bread.

"Nothing. I don't think we are going in the right direction. Something is missing, like an imprortant clue or a link. Things don't add up, you know." Aayat opened her palms and moved them sideways. Some dough fell on Feedaa's lap who gave a fake laugh and put it back.

"How come?"

"Look here." Aayat checked her chip and projected the notes and charts on the opposite wall. She seemed to be carting the charts with her all the time these days. "No connection between the events and disappearance. Only three of them happened on the days with specific planetary movements. The rest all happened on simple nights, I mean with no specific alignment of anything."

"Hmm." Feedaa looked at the gibberish details. Aayat had translated the notes in her language.

"You will find one. It takes only a moment for the breakthrough. I am sure you will get one." Feedaa then jumped off the counter and started the machine. Aayat still couldn't get a hang of how to use them and preferred Feedaa or Sae Sae handled the wares while she did the chopping, mincing as well as the dirty dishes after the meals. "How much have you learned about our world?" Feedaa questioned, placing the food in the radio wave cooker.

Sae Sae had asked her to prepare Aayat for the possibility that she might have to stay here longer. To assimilate, she needed to learn their ways of life. Even if she pretended to be mute and didn't talk to anyone, she had to know certain things. Errumm was working on procuring identification for her in the meanwhile.

"Well, I understand your time but not the calendar, your reference points are too many, and the lunar calendar seems confusing to me."

"Then how are you studying the disappearances? They are all marked by dates, right?"

"I have created my own calendar based on the dates that I remember."

"How?" Feedaa asked, switching off the cooker, which was blaring repeatedly, informing them of the job well done.

"I know when I came here, I mean the date on which I fell into the stream, and then there are some references in Sae

Sae's dad's journal. He had written the dates of our world in the journal when he went away for two months and learned our language. That happened around ten sun cycles ago, so I marked that date, and then according to the season and some help from Sae Sae, I could reach an approximate date, give or take fifteen days."

"That's such a tough thing to do." Feedaa picked one of the wraps Aayat had set on the plate and took a large bite. Aayat had blended the *iska* flour, she didn't like much, with vegetables and fruits of her choice, added a few herbs. It tasted different from what she was used to, but Feedaa liked trying new things.

"I didn't have anything else to do, either." Aayat shrugged her shoulders.

"How many sun cycles back did you go?"

"Around till the time of your birth." Aayat picked the other wrap, bit it and chewed slowly, using her fingers to clean the corner of her lips.

Feedaa swallowed her food and hooted.

"Can we please go out now? I am sick of being stuck here," Aayat asked as they devoured the second wrap and threw the plates in the sink. "I'll do the dishes when we are back."

Despite her reluctance to do so, Feedaa agreed.

In a crowded eatery in the centre of the town market, Ray sat at a table for two, waiting for Sae Sae to arrive. They had frequented the place when they were together. It smelled like fresh lavender. The owner placed flowers at every corner of the place. The smell reminded Ray of happier times.

"How have you been?" Sae Sae asked, sitting in front of her.

"Good, and you?"

"Good."

"Are you?" Ray asked. "You look tired." She traced his face with her gaze. Were it the old days, she would have touched his face and coaxed him into sharing his worries with her. But now, all she could do was look at him.

"Ray, is there a possibility that we have been mistaken in Amber's case?" Sae Sae took a sip of water.

"Mistaken?"

"What if she got lost in the woods, and we thought she crossed the portal?" Sae Sae's words sounded cruel. He was asking her to overturn almost five years of her work and belief.

"Why do you think so?" she asked, looking at a kid on the other table.

"I have been studying links between the cases, you know, what happened when and if there was anything out of the ordinary that accompanied the disappearances." He looked at her and licked his dry lips. "So there are three cases that happened during such phenomenon, but your sister's isn't one of them."

Ray drummed her fingers on the surface of the table. "You are still seeing people from Street twelve-one?"

Sae Sae looked at her and squinted. "You knew?"

"What is there that I don't know? Including the rumour that you are hiding a human." She straightened and looked at him.

His mouth fell open.

"Is it true? It is, isn't it?"

"Who are *you* talking to these days?" Sae Sae's face turned red.

"You were never good at deflecting, Sae Sae. You always get angry when something you are hiding gets out in public." She then leaned closer and said, "You know you can trust me. Even if we are on a break, you can still trust me. We have been through worse together."

"Why were you trying to get into Abee's study that day? You never go to places you aren't invited." Sae Sae shifted in his chair.

Ray looked at the counter. "When will our food get ready? I am really hungry. I ordered as soon as I came. Your favourite…"

"Someone asked you to do that. Didn't they?" Sae Sae held her chin lightly and moved it to make her face him. "Tell me what you are hiding."

"Only if you tell me what you are hiding." Despite the impulse to let his hand stay over her chin forever, Ray jerked her face, shaking his hand away. "Promise me you will keep me in the loop."

"Don't do that, Ray. You know it's no use." Sae Sae put his hand on the table.

"When will we be off this stupid break?" she asked.

"You—you . . ." he felt a loss of words.

"Yes. I was never with you because it gave me purpose. I was with you because I love you, and I still do. Despite all the differences and fights and anger, I cannot, I do not find the strength to let you go." Tears streamed down her face.

"Sorry," he said after a while.

"Don't be." She wiped the tears away. "I am not saying this to make you feel guilty or to force you to change your decision. I just thought you should know. You may take as much time as you want. I will still be here."

The number on the counter changed and Ray got up to get the order. Sae Sae scratched the cuticles of his index finger with his thumb. "Is there anything else I should know?" he asked as she returned with a food laden tray.

Ray nodded. "Some people contacted me to get your father's files. They said they just wanted to check if we were not doing anything illegal and also that they might be of help."

"Who?" He took the tray from her hands and placed it on

the table.

Ray took her seat and distributed the food between them.

"What did you say to them?" Sae Sae changed the question.

"I tried getting the papers, and when I couldn't they stopped contacting me."

"And then?" He nibbled the bread.

"We came to *this*," Ray moved her index finger between then, pointing at him and then at herself.

"Do these people or anyone of them has a name?"

"Jackal," she whispered.

Sae Sae's face contorted as he closed his fist tightly in anger. "I am going to kill him. How dare he approach you."

She tried calming him down. "It's okay, Sae Sae. They have a lot more information on the interregnum than we do. They are larger in number and a collective unit."

"Don't take their side," he snapped.

"I am not, but they are good at trading information."

"You shared something?"

She said in a matter-of-fact tone, taking a bite from the platter in front of her, "A little. They wanted your father's notes. Everyone is after them, you know."

"Fine, I will give you a copy of one of his journals." He rubbed his temple.

"And what do you want in exchange?"

"First, stop meeting them so frequently. It's not safe, and I am not comfortable with the idea of you in that dingy den." He straightened.

"You can't order me." Ray almost slammed the cup on the table.

"I didn't mean it that way. I am worried for your safety, and those are human lovers. They don't follow the rules."

She swallowed her food and asked, "What do you want in return, Sae Sae?"

"I have been studying the dates of the disappearance

closely these days. Three of them align with planetary configurations and release of natural energy or something of that sort. The others don't. I need to know what they know about that. I was hoping if you could ask around a little." He then suddenly changed his stance. "No, you don't need to do that. You are out for good. What was I even thinking? I will take care of all this. You stay away."

Ray smirked. "Since when have you become this distrustful? Just give me the notes, and I will get what you need. Let's meet in three days." She got up, paid the bill, and left.

CHAPTER EIGHTEEN

Sae Sae and Aayat were shoulders deep into notes. They ate, slept, breathed the data on the disappearances. Sae Sae rarely went out, and Aayat too hadn't taken a break. All they thought of was the connection between the disappearances, something that could have been verified. There were only so many days left until the siege, and it was proving to be difficult to get a fake identification card. Errumm was cutting several corners, keeping almost all her ethics at bay to help them.

"We need to look at the bigger picture."

"What?" Sae Sae asked without looking at Aayat.

"The natural phenomena. I still don't understand a lot about them. How is the energy generation opening the portal? Is it really that or are there other phenomena? How exactly does the portal open? Is there a particular frequency at which the molecules resonate to allow the passage? What exactly is the passage? Absorption and release like the body of the person is absorbed by the passage and then thrown in the other world—sort of osmosis-like phenomenon? How is it even possible? But then, I didn't walk here. How did I even cross the interregnum? What on earth is this interregnum? There is a lot I don't understand."

Neither did Sae Sae, but this was all Jackal had told Ray after taking his father's notes. It felt like a lost deal. He had given so much without gaining anything worthwhile in return, but there was no point crying now. They needed to make the most out of those words. Sae Sae's skin had almost sagged like an ageing man. He had bags under his eyes and his clothes were all but crumpled. His blue eyes carried a hint of red all the time as they overworked those days. His brain too was overworking.

"You do not seem well, why don't you take a break?" she suggested.

"I am going out for a while."

"Don't." Sae Sae stopped and looked at Aayat, who quickly listed the reasons. "It's hot. June is the hottest month in our world, and the sun is blazing with all its might in yours, too. Also, you are exhausted. Rest for a while, you cannot keep going like this. You are not a machine."

Sae Sae rubbed the nape of his neck. She had suddenly become too beautiful to resist. The heat rising inside him was threatening to overcome him.

"I will be in my room if you need me." He ran away from her as fast as possible.

Tenzen and Errumm worked full-time to manage the details of the siege. Only ten days were left until the full moon. They did not have a moment to spare. Everyone was ready in their positions. Old-style analog cameras were installed at all the places they could, while the rest were to be attached to the investigator's clothes. All the digital devices were abandoned lest they left any electronic footprints and alert the group beforehand. They had cross-checked and rechecked and then cross-checked the schedule of almost everyone living on street 12.1.

"Let's take a break for today," Errumm declared at almost midnight. "Everyone has worked hard. Go home and rest, we will catch up tomorrow."

The team members got up to leave when Tenzen whispered, "Errumm if you don't mind, I need to discuss something."

"Yeah, sure. What?" She gave a tired smile.

"Let everyone leave." He went ahead to pour himself a glass of water.

Once the room was empty, Tenzen half-stretched himself on the sofa and yawned. He then rubbed his face to wake himself for the conversation he was about to have.

Errumm warmed some leftovers from lunch and brought them to the table. "What was it that you wanted to talk about?"

"Let's eat first," Tenzen stuffed his mouth with food and grunted, chewing the meatballs as fast he could.

"I wish this would all end soon," Errumm said, looking into oblivion. "It's so tiring. I haven't slept properly in ages. Also, Feedaa needs her mother. We need to spend some time together. I am so thankful to Sae Sae for taking care of her, but still, he is a child himself."

Tenzen looked at her. A commanding officer, a caring superior, and a loving mother. Her image had changed so much in the past few days.

After they finished the food, Tenzen sat in front of her and said, "I am not sure how to say this, please don't take offence."

"Whatever it is, just say it clearly."

Tenzen cleared his throat. "There are rumours that your nephew is hiding a human in his bunker."

The expression on Errumm's face changed—anger, fear, shame.

Tenzen looked at her, his eyes narrowed. "It's okay, you do not have to confirm or explain anything. I am not looking for anything of that sort. I am just telling you because almost everyone is talking about this and also about taking you down in case all this is true."

Errumm remained silent.

"It's just that I wanted you to know that I am here if and

when you need me. Whatever be the case, I trust you, even though you asked me not to trust anyone, I still do." He then got up, collected his gadgets and files, and left.

Sae Sae came to the study after a few hours of sleep and was now hunched over the table, surrounded by old books, papers, and journals. Three different screens on the wall projected the information they had gathered on the disappearances.

Aayat was listening to an audio file when Sae Sae began murmuring, "Bigger picture, bigger picture, bigger picture."

"I really don't get why you keep repeating it day in and day out. It's not like repeating *bigger picture* all the time will lead you to it." Aayat closed the audio file.

"I don't know," he snapped.

"Let's start with the basics, then." She wiped the table clean and picked up a digital pen.

"How does a lunar eclipse occur?" she drew the picture of the phenomenon. The Sun and the moon on the opposite ends with the Earth in the middle, the shadow of Earth falling on the moon, covering its surface.

"What else?" She drew a question mark on the side of the figure.

Sae Sae sat up straight. "They are in a straight line. And when the Sun, Earth, and Moon are in a linear alignment, the tides are higher than usual as the energy of these three celestial bodies is in sync."

"Other than that, we have tidal wave generation which is unusually high when these three align in a straight line. Want to add anything?" She drummed the pen on the table.

"Energy generation, well, when waves crash into one another, they release energy, right?" He looked at her, not sure if his answer was good enough to be considered.

She bit her lower lip and tugged a tendril of her hair behind her ears.

"Bigger picture. Yes, maybe we should look for the phenomena that release energy or depend on a natural change in energy or entropy or something like that, or natural disasters?"

"Like volcano eruption, Flood, Tsunami, Avalanche." Sae Sae clapped his hands.

"Earthquake! Oh my God! Earthquake, Sae Sae, earthquake," Aayat jumped up and down in her chair. She then brought out the paper on which she had written the dates of her world along with the names of those who disappeared.

"This one, this person," she circled the fifth name on the list. "His disappearance date coincides with the earthquake whose epicentre was Kashmir, in late 2005."

"Slowly, slowly, say it slowly, so that I can also understand."

"Look, this date, let me first tally it with your calendar. The onset of winters, around the time when Feedaa would have been a year or two. Was there an Earthquake here?"

Sae Sae looked left and right as if searching for something and then replied, "I think there was some disturbance in the mountainous region. There were no severe casualties. My mother was one of the relief workers. Look." He showed her the picture he pulled from the web.

"One of the disappearances happened during this time." Aayat darkened the circle around the name.

They looked at each other and smiled.

"And one was almost a year before that, in the islands." Sae Sae checked news reports for natural disasters.

"That was a Tsunami, I don't know what you call it here."

"Wow!" Sae Sae exclaimed as they laughed like little children. Finally—the work was paying off.

They cross-checked every name on the list. Most

disappearances coincided with a natural phenomenon or disaster, an astronomical event, or cosmic energy release.

This news, though happy, left them both with thoughts.

Sae Sae thought of his father. These events were all opportunities for him to cross the interregnum, and yet he wasn't back. *What if he would never be back?*

Aayat, on the other hand, thought about Ray's sister, who still did not fit any of the categories.

What happened to that little girl?

Feedaa was watching an old video in the central area of the bunker when Aayat entered in the evening after a refreshing nap. The audjinn was spread on the sofa smiling ear to ear, munching something noisily. On the video, two Djinns, a grownup and a young kid, were racing. The older person seemed to lose purposely to the younger one, who looked at him angrily.

"Who are they?" Aayat asked, sitting beside Feedaa.

"Sae Sae and his dad." Feedaa slurped a thick, white liquid that seemed like a milkshake. "Want some?" she slid a bottle toward Aayat, who stared at the screen without blinking.

"What are you looking at?" Feedaa elbowed her.

"Something . . ." Aayat craned her neck forward and then for a few moments everything else seemed to have vanished, all she could see was the older Djinn.

"Are you all right?" Feedaa's voice reached her ears from afar.

Aayat licked her lower lip and looked at Feedaa. Her earpod allowed her to listen to the conversation between father and son in the video, and both voices were familiar. She then looked at the screen again.

"I think I have seen him before." Aayat went closer to the screen, still staring at it with wide eyes.

"Have you now?" Feedaa smirked.

"Yes."

"What did you say? *Who* have you seen?" Feedaa dashed closer.

"This person, I mean Sae Sae's dad. I think I may have seen him." Aayat bit her lower lip.

"Stop it. It's not funny." Feedaa turned off the projector.

"He has a burn mark on his right wrist, a small stem from which some thorn like things seem to grow." Aayat produced her wrist and drew the mark on it with her index finger.

"Yes, they were working on a semiconductor device—wait, how do you know?" Feedaa almost jumped.

"I saw it. He was tying his shoelace when I entered Doctor Khanna's office. He spoke in our language—but it seemed foreign on his tongue, I thought he was from some other country. I know it was him. He has the same eyes—oh my God, that's why Sae Sae's eyes looked so familiar. I remember telling my friend I haven't met someone with such blue eyes before." Aayat held her head in her hands and squatted on the floor.

"Where exactly did you see him?"

"At a conference at some university. I—um—I went there to listen to Doctor Khanna's lecture on the uses and design for language interpretation in artificially intelligent devices. I was quite impressed by his presentation and wished to talk more about it, so I went to talk to him further and there he was, I mean your uncle."

"Are you sure?" Feedaa whispered, slumping close by.

"Almost. But why was he there? What was he doing? How does he know Doctor Khanna? What the hell is happening?" Aayat's voice got louder with every word until she was shouting.

Feedaa looked as if she had seen a ghost, her face turned frost white. After a while of silence, she said, "Don't tell Sae Sae."

Aayat nodded and closed her eyes.

Chapter Nineteen

Amber's disappearance was turning out to be the most difficult case. She had disappeared almost five years ago. The video had aged and was of poor resolution. The gadgets weren't state of art at the time. Also, there was no clue of where she actually disappeared from. Everything was a hunch. Moreover, they could not trace any sign of terrestrial activity at the time of her disappearance. Finally, Sae Sae visited Ray's house, rang the bell, and called her out.

"Why was your sister in the jungle that night?" Sae Sae asked right at the door without so much as *hello*.

"Come again?" Ray was startled at his sudden visit to her house.

"Wasn't she too young to be wandering in that area alone? Why exactly was she there?" He moved her aside and entered the apartment.

She looked at him. "What do you mean?" Sae Sae's sudden interrogation made no sense. She stood in front of him, trying to hide the mess in the house. Mats were spread on the floor of the living room and her clothes were lying all over. Most of her gadgets were broken into bits and lay scattered.

"Ray, let's cut to the chase, okay. You know something that I don't." Sae Sae snapped, "And what the hell happened here?" He picked a broken semiconductor chip and turned it between his fingers.

"Have you come to trade information again? What are you giving this time?" Ray snatched the chip from him and kicked one of the cushions on the floor. There were so many things to ask about, so many unfinished conversations, but this was the reason he visited.

"Have you been working with those government haters all along?" he roared, looking all around the house, moving his head from side to side in succession.

"I only want my sister back."

"Isn't it too late to change sides now?" He picked a black cap with *12.1* embossed in peacock blue on it.

"I haven't changed sides, Sae Sae. You pushed me away." She was hurt, broken, and offended. Her voice turned hoarse.

"So, you went to the wrong ones." He waved the cap at her face.

"Leave. I don't want to see you ever again." She blinked her eyes to force back the tears lurking at the corner.

"What happened to your sister?"

"You doubt my story." Anger replaced her grief in a moment.

"Not at all, Ray. I know you, I trust you, I always have, but there is something missing, and for that, I need to know this." His expression mellowed, and his voice became soft. He brought his hand forward, near her cheeks, but then pulled it back.

"But you never asked this earlier."

"I thought she got lost." He placed his hand on the forehead and pressed hard.

"And so she did. She was a kid. We were all going through the trail of Kausar, and she might have seen something and ran after it. We never saw her again. We looked everywhere, at every nook and corner of the forest. The guard looked for a month. We went there repeatedly for almost a year, hoping to find her lying somewhere, but she had vanished," Ray said, as she wiped off a tear. "You already know all this. Why do you come here to torment me if there is nothing else to do?"

"Sorry, Ray. I really am sorry. I shouldn't have come here," he said as he turned to leave.

"You can come here anytime, Sae Sae, I hope you know that."

"I know, I know."

Sae Sae stood at the door of the dingy room he frequented at street 12.1. The room was crawling with numerous new faces, making Sae Sae angrier. He was tired, and anxious. Although things had started to unfold, they still could not link Ray's sister's case with the other disappearances. She had wandered off on a calm night, no rare phenomenon occurred on the day, as far as they could tell. Seeking Jackal was all Sae Sae could think of. He might have known something about Amber—he had to have something big enough to convince Ray to side with him. she wasn't the one to cross lines that easy.

Jackal saw him at the door and asked the others to leave. Several of them bumped into him on purpose and laughed when Sae Sae stared at them in anger.

"To what do I owe the honour?" Jackal asked as the last one left.

"Stop dragging everyone into your mess. Leave my people alone." The vein near Sae Sae's temple throbbed.

"Now, why would I do that?" Jackal's smile boiled Sae Sae's blood with rage. "Don't be so hard on yourself. I like you more when you are confident and smiling."

"What is it that you know, and I don't?" Sae Sae's eyes and ears turned hot. His toes curled inside his shoes.

"Why don't you take a seat first," Jackal said as he kicked a chair.

"I don't have time to entertain you," Sae Sae hissed, coming closer to the three-legged table they always sat around.

"Too bad. I like talking to you."

Sae Sae repeated the question, "What is it that you know

and I don't?"

"A lot. I have seasoned with age." The sly fox-like being leaned backwards into the chair.

Sae Sae slammed his fist on the table.

"Desperation makes us do things that we never think were possible." Jackal spoke in a calm voice, tracing his lower lip with his index finger in a playful manner.

"Stop giving me riddles in place of answers." Sae Sae bent over the table. Foam built around the corner of his mouth. He felt his shirt soak as sweat trickled down his spine.

"I am giving you the answer. Your rage isn't letting you see through it." Jackal scratched his chin with the index finger of his right hand as Sae Sae turned and left, ramming into the door on his way out.

Errumm awaited him at the parking of the bunker. She stood tapping her feet on the ground.

Sae Sae ran towards her, "I didn't know you were coming."

"Let's go inside first," she replied.

The two hurried in. Errumm led him straight to her brother's study and placed an identification card on the table and said, "This is for the human." She then looked at him, her eyes narrowed and said, "People know."

Sae Sae nodded, his shoulders stooped by the weight of the responsibility.

"Be safe," Errumm said after some time. "Do tell me if you need anything else. I'm always there for you." She then patted his shoulder, and left.

Sae Sae went downstairs. Aayat and Feedaa were having an animated conversation. He decided it was better not to show the identification card to Aayat yet. Giving it to her would mean he had lost all hope of sending her back. He had no intention of doing that to her sooner than he needed.

"Hey stranger," Feedaa waved at him.

"You are here again? Don't you have other people to disturb," he said as he walked towards the kitchen.

"Don't be so cruel," she said, throwing a pen lying nearby at him.

"What do you want to eat?" Sae Sae asked as he rolled his sleeves. "I'll cook anything you like." He then busied himself in peeling, slicing, chopping, dicing, and cooking.

The three of them had a wonderful night. They laughed, played games, ate, and talked till sunrise. Exhausted, they slept on the sofa and the easy chair.

Aayat was the first to wake up. She saw the two Djinns lying unconscious in strange postures and smiled. Who knew such a day would come in her life?

"Don't do that, it's creepy." Sae Sae opened his eyes. His voice startled Aayat, and she jumped, waking Feedaa in the process, who sprinted to her house as soon as she checked the time.

"Did you find anything out?" Aayat asked as they cleaned the kitchen after breakfast.

Sae Sae shook his head.

"It's okay, don't worry too much," she said, smelling the leftovers to check if they needed to go into the refrigerator or the trash can.

"Don't you want to go back home?"

She looked at him—his face, his hooked nose, the thin lips, and the slight chin. Everything about him was inviting. "Yes and no. I miss home—mom, dad, work, my fish, and the food, but . . ." She bit her lower lip and averted her eyes.

"But?" he seemed to want to hear more.

"I like it here, too."

He inched closer, shortening the distance between the two

and said, "Go on."

"Feedaa and you, I—never mind. Let's pay attention to the task at hand." She turned towards the sink and began scraping the plates. There was no time for distractions. They needed to focus. She needed to focus.

The tranquillity was interrupted by the sudden buzzing of the security alarm in the lab. It was strange. No one came there. The place was almost in the jungle.

The security sensor blared continuously. It could have been anything or anyone.

They ran to the monitor and checked the footage of the camera at the gate. The inspection team was preparing to enter the lab. Aayat's mouth dried instantly. She looked at Sae Sae, who stared at the screen without moving. She shook his shoulder lightly. No response—he seemed to be in a trance. She called his name, but he wouldn't budge. Suddenly, he exhaled sharply, held her wrist, and whispered, "We need to get out of here, now."

CHAPTER TWENTY

Sae Sae was sure they would have come after them wherever they might have run to, but staying in the bunker would do them no good, either. The choice to run to the city or towards the jungle was equally dangerous. They crept into the basement, then went to Sae Sae's room, where a tiny opening led to an underground tunnel that opened a kilometre and a half away from the bunker. They moved the cupboard hiding the opening and tip-toed out of the place as silently as they could.

There was an old workshop Sae Sae used to frequent to get his gadgets remodelled when he didn't know about them as much. He ran in that direction. It had been closed for months. Sae Sae looked around, but the door but was jammed. He shook the door violently, trying to open it. They were out of breath and scared. When nothing worked, Sae Sae summoned all his strength and punched one of the windowpanes, but nothing happened. Lucky for them, the laser detectors were turned off, as the place had been empty for so long.

Aayat scratched her head repeatedly, making him furious.

"Stop that and think of a way to get out," he whispered angrily, but received no reply.

"Why don't you have wooden doors with knobs?" Aayat kicked the screen of the door, which unlatched slightly, making her lose her balance.

Sae Sae leapt into action and placed his foot between the door and the wall, lest it closed again. "How did you do that?" he asked, perplexed, and pushed the door with all his might, making enough space for one person to get in sideways. They crept in somehow. Once inside, they slumped on the floor.

The heat was sweltering. Despite the sweat and greasy, itchy skin, the two maintained their positions. They were cramped in a small corner, trying not to even breathe the wrong way. There were cameras everywhere, and no one could be trusted.

"What now?" Aayat whispered into his ears.

"Can't say. We need to inform aunt Errumm, but we have no means to do that, either."

"Isn't there anything here that you could use to send a signal?"

"They might be tracing it."

"It's a risk we have to take. If nothing works, you can hand me over and say I was staying with you by force," Aayat said in a matter-of-fact way, which made Sae Sae's heart pound with fear.

He craned his neck to see outside, but everything was pitch black. The day had turned into a long, unending night. He dared not switch on the lights. Crawling a little, he moved out of the confinement to look for a way to communicate. His stomach growled.

There was an old communication device covered with dust. He took it in his hands and dusted it off. Scared of getting caught, he tucked it away, but his mind went back to it repeatedly. It was their only hope. They could not stay in the workshop forever. They needed help.

Sae Sae placed the device in his pocket. He would think about reviving it later, but first they needed to move. Staying at a place for too long was equally dangerous. Aayat was half dozing by then. A part of him wanted her to relax a bit, but the other part debated that the dead of the night was the best time to slip out of the place. He jabbed Aayat's shoulder with his finger to wake her up, gestured her to follow and turned to the broken door. He had placed his shoe there in order to keep it open.

"Where are we going?" Aayat whispered, rubbing her eyes.

"To the jungle."

They stepped out of the door. Sae Sae peered around. It was eerily quiet, not even the sounds of crickets could be heard. *This can't be. There has to be a catch.* He looked again, but there was no trace of anyone. Whatever the case, they had to hurry.

He held Ayat's hands tightly and inched towards the jungle. Crawling, peeking in the dark, trying to make sense of their surroundings, they reached the stream. Its gurgling noise filled the wide expanse of the jungle.

On the other side of the stream, Jackal awaited with his gang. Ray stood by his side.

"Hello there, Sae Sae, she must be the human you are trying too hard to protect." He looked at Aayat and grinned.

The moon was shining with all its might. Startled by the sudden meeting, Aayat shrieked. Sae Sae clasped his hand over her mouth. Her eyes widened. However, when she started hyperventilating, he moved his hand and loosened his grip. Aayat looked around, anxious to find a way to get away. She could hear several footsteps rushing towards them. The district officials were there. She needed to do something. When nothing came to her mind, Aayat ran towards the stream. She could hear Sae Sae following close behind, shouting for her to stop, but she was going crazy. She could not let others hurt Sae Sae because of her. She needed to get as far away from him as possible. She was the one everyone was after. Once she was gone, everything in his life would go back to normal. He could make an excuse, any excuse for her presence in his bunker and negate any association they had.

She looked at the moon desperately. She could hear her heartbeat.

Suddenly the stream became violent. The soft flowing water heaved mightily up and down, each wave several meters high. Some water splashed on her. It seemed inviting.

She took a last look at Sae Sae. She had to do everything in her power to save him.

"No, Aayat no. Please no, Aayat don't." She could hear his faint cries.

The stream was still raging. She plunged into it, hoping to get swept, but instead, she saw a surge of light gushing in from all sides. She closed her eyes and loosened her body, allowing nature to take its course.

And then everything turned black.

Absolute black.

To be continued . . .

About Nazia

Born and raised in Dehradun, a valley in the Himalayas, Nazia fell in love with writing at a young age. Her work can be read online on FemAsia, Rigorous, The Whorticulturalist, The Bright Flash Literary Review, Indus Women Writing as well as in several anthologies.